Praise for *If Thy Ri*

"Lamont has treated a painful and difficult subject within the context of an enthralling mystery. A superb first novel."
—SUSPENSE MAGAZINE

"This is a splendid debut novel from a promising author."
—MYSTERY TRIBUNE

"Exploring the volatile treatment of sex offenders vs. society and the real-time challenges of Asperger's Syndrome, Lamont carves a coherent and thoughtful path through often emotionally loaded territory with a bounty of relevant material — a thoughtful balance of crime and punishment."
—LUAN GAINES, Contributing Editor, *Curled up With a Good Book*

Praise for *Wright for America*

"Snappy dialogue and a madcap pace propel this lighthearted caper... Lamont who has performed on Broadway and worked as an assistant district attorney, clearly knows the territory, and her fast-paced high enjoyable novel is all the better for it."
—PUBLISHERS WEEKLY

"For anyone who has ever longed to see one of those hatemongering, rightwing blowhards get their comeuppance, Robin Lamont's Wright for America is that revenge fantasy come to print. The author has crafted a delightful, if at times wacky, tale that will leave her audience with a satisfied smile on their faces."
—FOREWORD REVIEW

"What a find! Too many characters will be familiar to us wonks, but it makes it all that more fun. Ever want to see the bloviating bubble busted? Step Wright up."
—POLITICAL CARNIVAL

THE KINSHIP SERIES

THE
CHAIN

DISCARD

ROBIN LAMONT

Award winning author of *If Thy Right Hand*

Cover and Interior Design: AuthorSupport.com
Cover Imagery: Shutterstock/Bernhard Richter

Grayling Press

ISBN: 978-0-9858485-4-5

LCCN: 2013946532

Printed in the United States of America

ACKNOWLEDGEMENTS

This book would not have been possible without Gail Eisnitz – a pioneer in the animal protection world. Her book *Slaughterhouse*, was transformative for me, changing forever the way I see our relationship with animals. Gail's help with the manuscript has been invaluable, as is her friendship.

My gratitude also to Martin Rowe of Lantern Books for his wisdom and encouragement and for setting me on the path of The Kinship Series. To Paul Shapiro, thanks for being such a staunch supporter. Thanks also to Dr. Shiya Ribowsky, Amanda Hitt, and to Jason Spector for their counsel and expertise.

For Ken Swensen, my selfless editor and husband, I could not do this without you. Your patience, persistence, and commitment to helping animals is a constant inspiration.

Finally, I am grateful to investigators Cody Carlson and "Pete" for taking me inside the world of slaughterhouses and factory farms.

The Chain is dedicated to all the undercover investigators who risk their lives, health, and sanity to shine
a light on some of the darkest places on earth.

Chapter 1

Frank Marino tightened his hands around the old laptop computer, wondering if his arthritic fingers had the will to part with it. The plastic casing was battered and scratched, but the hard drive held something invaluable. It held the truth – hours of secret recordings for which he'd risked everything. In a few minutes it would be lost forever.

Someone must have seen him and gone straight to Warshauer, who hadn't made a straight out threat. He only said, "You have to think about Verna and Sophie." Funny thing was when Frank first strapped on the hidden camera he *was* thinking about them. They deserved a better husband and father – a man who had principles. He'd tried to go through channels. After years of management giving him the brush-off, he'd written letters to the USDA, to OSHA, and the State Attorney General's office ... no response. Nothing. Not even *acknowledge receipt of your letter*. Screw them. He went on the internet and bought the spy camera. Just maybe he could do something that would reduce the suffering of the animals and the workers. Just maybe he could get his dignity back.

At least that's what he was thinking until they found out.

He squinted through his car windshield into the darkness, expecting headlights at any moment. *Bring everything, wait here,* they said. Some computer geek from corporate wanted to see the footage. Probably delete it right then and there. Frank ran his tongue over his dry lips, dying for a drink. Then he closed his eyes while failure washed over him and worked its way into his bones.

A knock on the window startled him. A man motioned for Frank to unlock the passenger door, then slid in. He wore shiny leather gloves and carried an attaché case. Dark blond hair, clean shaven and well-dressed down to his Gucci loafers, he looked too sharp to be a tech nerd, Frank thought. Guys like this always made him feel stubby and dark-skinned, the way he remembered his Italian grandfather.

"You're making the right decision, Frank," the man said in an oddly collegial fashion. "You bring it?"

"Yeah."

"Okay, let me see."

Frank unclenched his fingers and handed over the laptop. "What's your name?" he asked as the man powered it up.

"Bloom," was all he said. *Bloom* – first name, last name? Just before getting started, Bloom reached into an inside pocket of his jacket, took out a silver flask and drew a gentlemanly pull. As he re-corked it, Frank's eyes locked onto the flask then flickered to the glove compartment.

Bloom noticed and said, "You don't need an invitation from me."

And because Frank wanted the alcohol more than he resented the stranger's ability to see through him, he reached over and retrieved the pint of Jim Beam he kept for emergencies – that's what he called it anyway. His wife took a dim view of the habit, accusing him of having *emergencies* every day based on the number of empty bottles she found in the trash. He was trying to cut back ... but now was not the time. A little hair of the dog would settle his nerves. Frank unscrewed the cap, breaking the seal, and took a long drink. He felt the reassuring burn and wiped his mouth with the back of his hand.

"This it?" asked Bloom, as the first shaky images came up on the computer screen.

"Yeah." Frank looked away to avoid seeing the file deleted and with it a part of his soul, both about to be dispatched to an indifferent, black universe from which they could not be retrieved.

"Camera?" asked Bloom curtly.

Frank fumbled in his jacket pocket and removed the miniature video recorder. He gave it over to Bloom, who packed it in his attaché case crisply, matter-of-factly, like an exec wrapping up a business meeting.

"Okay, how about copies?" Bloom asked. "Surely you made a copy."

"Nope." Frank took another slug from the bottle.

"No?" Bloom pressed amiably.

"I said no, goddammit."

"Okay, then. Any questions?"

"Damn straight," said Frank. "No one goes near my wife and daughter, right?"

"Of course not. Not if you're giving me everything."

Frank screwed up as much bravado as he could. "If anything happens to either of them, I'll kill you," he said flatly.

Bloom glanced at him with a mixture of curiosity and pity, and Frank curled his fist into a ball. But suddenly feeling weak, he covered his anger the only way he knew – by taking another drink.

"How did they find out I was taping?" he asked.

"Someone saw you with the camera inside," replied Bloom coolly. "We were curious what you planned to do with it, so we got your cell phone from your locker and put in a piece of spyware."

Frank shook his head in disbelief. "Shit. So you know about the girl? You listened to all our conversations?"

"We did."

A chill went down the back of Frank's neck. "I'm supposed to meet with her tomorrow." It must have been the bourbon on an empty stomach, but an overwhelming sleepiness was trying to lock down his brain. He shook the fog from his head and tried to reassure the man. "Look, I'm not going to risk ... I'll make something up, tell her I changed my mind ... I won't say a word." The sound of his own voice seemed to be coming from far away.

"Of course not," Bloom replied. "Listen Frank, I've got a question for *you*. How did you get the conversation on tape?"

"What?" It was so close in the car, Frank struggled for air. He tried to take a deep breath, but his chest felt constrained by a slowly tightening band.

"I said how did you get Bannerman and your boss Warshauer on tape?"

"Crawl space. Sent me down there. Rats. Too many rats, gotta put ... poison ... in the ducts."

Bloom nodded in understanding. Sure, there must be air ducts running through the offices that ended in the crawl space below the building. A ten or twelve inch duct would probably magnify the sound of people speaking in the office upstairs – and there was Frank recorder-ready. Incredible. A perfect shit-storm.

Frank wanted to impress on Bloom that neither his wife nor daughter knew anything about it. But something had gone terribly wrong and he couldn't think of the words. So tired. The bottle slipped out of his hand and fell between his legs, spilling out the last two inches of whiskey on the floor mat. He gripped the steering wheel and managed to fire off a final salvo. "You people are ... scumbags. All of you, Warshauer, Bann'man, and fuckin' Seldon Marsh..."

"That's not my area," said Bloom, watching him carefully.

"Whuss your *area?*"

Frank's heart slowed to a death march beat, his skin was cold and clammy, he could barely breathe. Unable to fight anymore, he rested his forehead on the steering wheel and let himself be pulled into the black.

"This," said Bloom. He waited a few more moments until he knew that Frank wasn't coming back. "This is my area."

And then he got to work.

Chapter 2

Alice Chapel blew a lock of hair from her face while she flipped the bacon with one hand and reached for a stack of plates with the other. The sun was just beginning to lift itself above the tree line behind the house. Streaks of light filtered in through the cramped window of the small, wood-paneled kitchen and fell on the smiling snapshots affixed to the refrigerator with magnets. Frantic cartoon voices blared from the TV in the next room, and as she laid down the plates and plastic glasses, she called out to Will again.

Her youngest finally turned off the TV and bounced into the kitchen with his six-year-old curiosity in full gear.

"Am I going on a school trip today?" he asked, pulling out a chair from the table and perching precariously on the edge.

"No, honey, that's next week," said his mom.

"Why can't it be today?"

"Because they didn't schedule it for today, they scheduled it for next week." She spooned some scrambled eggs onto his plate and poured him a glass of orange juice.

Will thought about it for a moment, then said with finality, "It should be today."

His father, who had overheard, came into the kitchen and went right for the coffee. "You can bring that up with the superintendant when you get to school," he advised his son.

"What's a super attendant?" asked Will.

"A school official with a cape," said Emmet, taking his seat.

"Is that so he can fly?"

"Yeah – fly the school budget under the town's radar."

Alice put a plate of eggs and bacon in front of her husband. "Let him eat his breakfast, Emmet," she scolded. "Eat your eggs, Will, they're getting cold." She went into the hallway and called to Caroline to hustle up.

Back in the kitchen, neither of her boys had touched their breakfast. "Eat, eat," she pressed Will. Then she looked at Emmet.

"I'm not hungry," he said.

"No surprise," replied Alice, her lips pressed tight with disapproval.

He tilted back in his chair, working on his coffee and staring out the window.

"These are too runny," complained Will, lifting a spoonful of wet egg and letting it plop back onto his plate.

"Fine," said Alice tersely. She snatched both breakfasts away from the table and set them on the counter. "Eggs are nearly two dollars a dozen, so the both of you can eat this tonight. Will, go and get your shoes and don't forget your backpack."

When he trudged off, she sat down across from her husband. Alice had fallen in love with Emmet Chapel at age sixteen, and he was all she ever wanted. Now, she saw him red-eyed and hung over – a frequent condition that threatened to uproot the firm soil that held the family together. It made her furious at the same time it was breaking her heart.

Caroline came in and made a beeline for the coffee maker. As usual, their sixteen-year-old daughter was dressed inappropriately for school – no coat, not even long sleeves on this cold October morning, her black skirt too short, her gray top too tight. She was inches taller than Alice and had her father's striking features, though she seemed to be doing everything possible to negate them. She wore thick stripes of black eyeliner and had chopped off her long brown hair, refusing to go to a salon so they could trim the shaggy edges. Infuriating her parents further, she had pierced her nose to complement her multiple ear piercings. At home, disdain was her trademark and she clutched it to her chest the way she carried her school books.

After pouring herself a cup of coffee, Caroline leaned against the counter, daring her mother to suggest food. Alice was too smart for that and didn't even try. But Emmet's buttons were more easily pushed.

"You're not going out in that, I hope," he said.

Pretending she hadn't heard, Caroline blew on her coffee.

"You have gym clothes at school?" he demanded. "Because you're not doing track in that ridiculous outfit."

"I'm not on track anymore," she stated.

"What?"

"I said I'm not doing track. I quit."

Emmet's jaw muscles rippled with anger. "Why the hell did you do that?"

"Because there's no *point*," she shot back.

Emmet growled, "Don't start that again."

Alice tried to head off another fight. "They have to get to school," she said weakly.

But her daughter was ready for a clash. "And don't you tell me what I can or can't believe," she burst out. "A lot of predictions have come true. And it's not so far fetched when you consider global warming–"

"It's ridiculous, Caroline," he spat angrily. "This is some kind of sick, romantic fantasy you have – and I'm tired of it."

The teen had fire in her eyes. She thrust her face forward and clenched her fists. "Dad ... you are so out of touch with the universe that you wouldn't see the truth if it drove a truck."

"Caroline, please, honey..." Alice was crying now.

"I'm sorry it makes you sad," Caroline said, holding her ground. "For your information, it makes me sad, too. At least let me have these last months without fighting all the time." She was close to tears herself.

Emmet slammed his coffee cup down in frustration. "This is all because of that boy – that long-haired, tattooed freak."

"He is not a freak!"

"And he does drugs," added Emmet bitterly.

"No, he doesn't. He smokes a little weed. Big deal. Everybody at school does."

"Oh, great!" Emmet stood up, scraping his chair against the linoleum floor with a piercing screech. "I'm going to work," he said and stormed out.

Alice called after him, "I thought Frank was picking you up." But the door had already slammed behind him.

Outside there was a thin layer of frost blanketing his car. Emmet slid into the driver's seat and turned on the ignition, hoping the junk heap would start one more time. Screw Frank if he couldn't show up on time. His head pounded as he grasped the ice cold wheel and his eyes moved to his hands. There was still a thin line of darkened blood under a couple of fingernails. Jesus, would it never come out? Then he caught a glimpse of himself in the rearview mirror and zeroed in on the pronounced scar that ran from under his left eye, across his temple, and into his hairline. Its pale sheen of new skin drew attention to his electric blue eyes, the ones Caroline had inherited. Emmet Chapel used to be handsome. But it wasn't the injury that marred his good looks. It was what happened when you turned into a man you never wanted to be – never imagined yourself to be. The booze dulled that knowledge. But this thing with Caroline kept bringing it back to life, kicking and screaming.

CHAPTER 3

The pastor's voice rolled sonorously over the mourners, but all Emmet could hear was the creak of the ropes as they rubbed against the wood. He and Howard Bisbee held tight the supporting lashes at one end of the casket and two of Verna's cousins held the others, suspending it over the yawning, cold-blooded cavity. When the pastor's voice rose to deliver the last line of the psalm, Bisbee locked eyes with Emmet, who nodded, and they began to deliver Frank Marino's body into the earth. The others followed suit, hand over hand, lowering the coffin as gently as they could until it bumped on the bottom. And in those moments, the last conversation he had with Frank at the bar replayed in Emmet's head.

.... He and a couple of the guys were at their regular table knocking off a pitcher of beer when he spotted Frank walk in and take the only empty stool at the bar. The place was always crowded on a Friday night; just about everybody congregated at the Lazy Cat after their shifts at D&M Processing. No one could remember what the D stood for, but the M was for Marshfield. As for the "processing" – that was an industry euphemism for slaughterhouse. Emmet held up his hand and waited to see if Frank would signal, a wave or eye contact, but nothing. As soon as the stool next to him opened up, Emmet swallowed his irritation and made the first move.

"Hey," said Emmet, sidling onto the vacated bar stool.

Frank's shoulders were hunched, making his stocky frame look even more rounded, and he stared straight ahead with a glower on his face that normally spelled trouble.

Emmet caught the bartender's eye, pointed to Frank's drink and held up a finger.

The gesture seemed to do the trick because Frank finally turned to Emmet. "How's Caroline doing?" he asked.

"Still fixated on premonitions and whatever. If she was younger I'd put her over my knee and spank the bejesus out of her."

"It'll pass."

"Better hope so. This shrink wants to put her on some kind of anti-depressant and insurance don't cover it on account of it's *psychological*. Costing me a fortune. You want to come sit at the table with us?"

"I'm not staying," said Frank. "I got an appointment."

"*Appointment*? Who with?"

Frank sized up his friend for a moment before shrugging. "Some day I'll tell you about it." Then he stared above the bar to a TV screen where the Panthers were playing. "Be nice if they could put together a season over five hundred."

Emmet knew he was trying to keep the conversation non-confrontational – anything to avoid addressing Emmet's promotion. "Ah, come on, Frank. Why can't you be happy for me?" he asked, unwilling to let it go. "I've been in line for this job for over a year. If they'd have offered it to you, you would've taken it."

"In the next life," scoffed his friend.

"It's my chance to get out."

"To get out?" Frank turned to him with his face set. "This doesn't get you out. It digs you in deeper. You have no freakin' idea who you're dealing with. Besides, you're not yellow hat material."

"The fuck I'm not."

"You're not, and I'll tell you why. Because you're not a leader, Emmet, you're a follower. You go with the path of least resistance. You always have."

"That's bullshit. And anyway, it's better than whining about every damn thing that happens at D&M," Emmet replied hotly. "If your wife wasn't friends with Patty Warshauer, you'd a'gotten fired a dozen times over. You're trying to buck the system, which changes nothing. And you don't have the balls to quit. Keep filing complaints with the USDA and you'll be cleaning worm-infested pig intestines for the rest of your goddamn life."

Frank's answering smile was filled with such self-reproach that for a moment, Emmet wished he could take his words back. But then Frank twisted the knife a little deeper. "Maybe so. But I'll say it again, you're not yellow hat material. As floor supervisor, you're gonna have to suck up to Warshauer and LaBrie and the rest of the USDA shits protecting their own asses. You're gonna have to write up your friends and keep the line moving so corporate can squeeze us for the extra buck. And frankly, you won't be able to cut it."

"Yeah? Why not?"

"'Cause in your heart you know it ain't right."

Emmet slammed down his beer and got up. "Screw you," were his parting words.

"I've been screwed my whole life," responded Frank. "Why should tonight be any different?" He drained the last of his drink and counted out a few bills on the bar before slipping off the stool and disappearing.

.... Emmet's thoughts returned to the present and all at once, he felt sick from the cloying scent of condolence flowers mounded on top of the coffin. He stepped back to take hold of Verna's hand, but Frank's wife stared past him at the rectangular hole in the earth, her grief hardening in a place he could not touch. Alice huddled near the girls who had their teenage arms locked around one another. Emmet looked around for his son, but Will had long since been commandeered by the antics of an older boy.

Emmet whispered harshly for Will to rejoin the family and took a knee to lecture him about proper behavior at a funeral. Going through the motions of fatherly discipline was his only distraction from the guilt. Frank had been his closest friend, and he'd carry their last bitter words forever.

Alice came over, fatigue and anxiety etched on her face. "Don't be hard on him, Emmet. It was a long service." She took Will by the hand. "Come on, honey. We're going to the house now."

"Our house?" he asked.

"No, Uncle Frank's house. Emmet, we're going with Verna and the girls."

"I'll be along in a minute."

He went back to the open grave and stood next to Howard Bisbee, who had his head bowed. Bisbee was a big man, awkward in his ill-fitting suit, and was one of the only black quality assurance technicians at D&M.

"Last week he had to put out rat poison underneath the

building," said Bisbee, without lifting his head. "I made a joke about it and he called me a prick."

"He called everyone a prick – at some point," said Emmet.

"I can't tell you why, exactly, but it kinda hurt my feelings."

"He didn't *think* you were a prick, Howard. He liked you."

"He could be a real difficult sonofabitch, but I liked him, too." Bisbee turned to go.

Emmet waited until everyone else had gone and stood by the freshly turned earth. It was the least he could do. At one point he looked up into the cloud-streaked sky and caught sight of a girl ... a woman on top of a small hill in the cemetery, sitting with her arms clasped around her knees on the cold ground. He had seen her mid-way through the service and hadn't paid much mind, assuming she was a visitor to one of the graves on the hill. But she was still there, looking down at Frank's casket. Her long hair, more amber than red, blended with the early fall colors of the trees.

Feeling as though he had to outlast her, Emmet closed his eyes and said the Lord's Prayer quietly, as much for himself as for his friend. When he looked up again, she was gone.

*   *   *

Leave the man in peace, thought Jude. She dusted off her backside and headed down the far side of the slope with his image etched in her mind. A lonely figure standing by the gravesite, he must be a relative or close friend. He seemed protective of Frank's wife, who was fairly easy to pick out – a stoic, sturdy woman in a black veil.

The girls had drawn her attention as well. Jude guessed that one of them, the heavier of the two, was Frank's daughter, looking like her mother as she did. The other girl was slim and long-legged and she offered comfort with a best friend's tender hugs rather than the fierce, grief-stricken clasp of a sibling. It was clear to Jude that their friendship went beyond liking the same music and the same celebrities. They needed each other.

Jude had parked her old but trusty Subaru station wagon near the cemetery's entrance. As she opened the car door, she saw Finn draped across the front seats. He raised his head and thumped his tail in guilty admission. "Back," she commanded, jerking her thumb in the direction of the cargo area. With practiced surrender, her dog managed to squeeze his large frame between the seats and move into the back. "How many times do I have to tell you, no front seat until you've passed your driving test," Jude scolded softly as she scratched him behind the ears. Finn leaned his head contentedly into her hand.

She pulled out onto the main street that ran through Bragg Falls. It was a rural, working town with a few local farms scratching at the edges. Until the 1950's it survived as a wholesale supplier of Christmas trees, and when the abundant land was turned into a state park, the town would've gone under if Marshfield hadn't brought in the meat packing plant. Most of the recreational action centered around the shopping mall over on Route 192, where there was a Walmart, a movie theater and a bowling alley. But here on Main Street, there were just local businesses and a handful of empty store fronts that had "for rent" signs in the windows. Jude drove slowly through the town center, looking from side to side as she passed the Post Office, a liquor store, and a red brick hardware store that sold feed and agricultural products. Next to it was the diner where she was to have met Frank Marino. Her last communication with him had been on Thursday night; she had planned to spend a couple of days here, taking his statement and going over the footage, maybe talking to other workers ... but now? The immediate future wasn't clear, though she knew one thing – she couldn't go back empty handed, not again.

A quarter of a mile further, over the railroad tracks, she spotted the Bragg Falls Motor Inn and navigated into the gravel parking lot. The motel was a row of low-roofed connected rooms, referred to on the neon sign as "guest suites." Each had an identical blue door and differed only by its proximity to the soda machine planted midway down the row. Jude found the office in the owner's house at the end of the row. Beyond a makeshift counter in the entryway was a living room where the owner sat on a sofa watching television. Catching sight of the new customer, the woman hoisted her two-hundred-pound frame and shambled to the counter. The trip cost her some labored breathing, but she welcomed her guest with a big smile.

"How can I help ya, honey?" she asked, taking stock of the tall, slender woman in front of her. Jude had pale, almost translucent skin and dark hazel eyes. Her face was heart-shaped with high cheekbones and an angular chin. Some might have said she had a Jane Eyre-like plainness, but if the light caught her in a certain way, the same people would have said she was quite beautiful.

"Do you take dogs?" inquired Jude.

The manager's smile dimmed, but briefly; she only had two guests at present, so she slid a sign-in sheet over toward Jude. "I guess it's okay."

Jude began to fill in the register. Name – Jude Brannock. Address – 110 Sanctuary Road, Washington, D.C. It wasn't her home address – she never gave that – but the offices of The Kinship, a non-profit that conducted investigations into animal cruelty. Sanctuary Road was named for a Jesuit parish long since gone, but Jude always thought it was right that the organization should land there.

The manager handed her a key. "What brings you to the Falls, honey?" she asked.

"A little work," said Jude.

"How long you gon' be with us?"

"Probably just the night."

"Well, enjoy your stay now."

Jude took Finn around back to stretch his legs and relieve himself. She hoped the owner wasn't looking out her back window or she might have regretted her decision. He was a large dog, weighing in at about ninety-five pounds, all muscle and brown and black fur, a mixed breed of strong, steady dogs. His size could be intimidating, but only, Jude thought, to those who overlooked the doleful, patient look in his eyes. Of course, if he felt threatened, that look quickly changed.

Jude unloaded the wagon and let Finn explore the room. She knew it was more than curiosity; he needed to know where the exits were before he could settle down. To Jude, motel rooms all looked the same, this one furnished with a bed, a side table, desk, and an open kitchenette with a mini refrigerator. From the smell of the place, the no smoking policy was not strictly enforced, but it wasn't the worst she had stayed in. She put out a bowl of water for Finn and settled in cross-legged on the bed to phone in.

CJ picked up. "What's happening, girl?"

"I'm here in Bragg Falls. Where's Gordon?" she asked, referring to their boss, Gordon Silverman.

"He's at a conference in New York. You meet your contact?" CJ Malone manned the phones in the office and conducted almost all the intelligence gathering that couldn't be done in the field. A childhood spine injury had put him in a wheelchair for life, but with his computer skills he had the world at his fingertips.

"CJ, he's dead."

"Say what?"

"He's dead." Jude could hardly believe it herself. "I was supposed to meet him in town this morning, but he never showed. I found his address in the phone book, and when I got there, there was a whole caravan of cars heading out. A neighbor told me that they were going to his funeral."

"Holy shit. What happened?"

"The neighbor said it was a drug overdose. I don't know any details yet." She pushed a stray wisp of hair behind her ear and tried to massage the anxious crease that had settled on her brow. "CJ, this is a real blow for us. Frank Marino had nearly three hours of video footage, date-stamped over a six-week period. He had workers constantly using electric prods, beating the hogs – a ton of Humane Slaughter Act violations."

"Wow, we could use slaughterhouse footage."

"Not only that, when I spoke with him last, he told me he had just gotten something on tape that could be extremely valuable to us. He didn't go into detail; all he said was that he had recorded a conversation between the plant manager, a guy name Bob Warshauer, and Ned Bannerman."

"Bannerman's the regional VP. What were they saying?"

"He told me that it implicated Seldon Marshfield himself and that it was potential dynamite. I didn't press him because I thought I'd talk to him when I got here. But now, Marino's dead and I don't have the tape. Even if I did, it doesn't have the same value – there's no one to authenticate it. We've been down this road. Marshfield will say it's fabricated, it wasn't taken at their facility, or you know the spiel ...'This is an isolated incident by workers who are not following our safe and humane procedures. We have zero tolerance' ... blah, blah, blah. I feel terrible about this. I got the feeling that Marino was a real fighter and he obviously risked everything to–"

"Hang on a second," interrupted CJ. "I've got Gordon on the other line."

Jude plucked at a frayed edge on the bed's comforter, trying to digest the disappointment. Was this going to be yet another embarrassment? Her last investigation into a doping scheme by trainers and vets in the horse-racing business was a bust after her informant reneged. He'd provided pages of information about horses being shot up with steroids, more than a dozen of them succumbing to heart attacks. But at the last minute he wouldn't sign off on any of it, claiming that Jude – the over-zealous animal activist – had arm-twisted him into saying things that weren't true. Word around the animal welfare community was that someone had paid off the informant, but it was accompanied by an undercurrent of buzz that she hadn't vetted the guy properly to begin with. For Jude, whose work meant everything to her, that hurt.

CJ got back on the line and told her to hang up, that Gordon would call her back. While she waited, she unpacked her duffel and set up her laptop, reading glasses and Marshfield files in a neat pile on the desk.

The phone rang. "Where is it?" was Gordon's first question.

"I don't know."

"Did he tell anybody else about the video?"

"I asked him to keep it under wraps until I got here, and when I spoke with him Thursday he was still employed, so management couldn't have known about it."

"How are *you* doing?" asked Gordon. He was all business when it came to animal protection, but thought of his staff as family. Gordon had been her lifeline to a stable adulthood – although she wondered sometimes how stable anything was in this type of work. Until she met him, she'd been floundering. No surprise given her scattered childhood, bounced from one foster home to another. Some of them were bad, and by the time she was in middle school Jude was adept at running away, believing she was safer on her own even if it meant living on the street.

The night that would draw her to Gordon and his work uncovering and exposing animal abuse was burned into her psyche. She was fourteen and occasionally hung out at a truck stop off the Turnpike. When things were slow, a late-shift waitress named Eve used to give Jude leftovers and let her sleep for a few hours in her car. This night, Jude was curled up under Eve's winter coat when she was awakened by strange noises. Slowly surfacing into consciousness, she tried to figure out what the sounds were ... grunting, shuffling, an occasional high-pitched squeal. She'd never heard anything like it before. She sat up and rubbed the condensation from the car window to peer outside. But there was nothing to see, just another big truck that had pulled up about ten feet away. The sounds were coming from inside.

She got out of the car and made her way tentatively to the eighteen-wheeler. There was a man in the cab with his head tilted back and his mouth open, snoring. Jude walked silently past him to the rear load, where steel walls punctuated with open vents rose up above her and the grunts and cries became more distinct. Smells, too, manure and urine. She reached up and put her fingers in one of the lower vents and pulled herself up on tiptoes. Putting her face close to the opening, she peeked in. A pair of dark, frantic eyes met hers and she fell back in alarm. *What the hell was that?* When she'd caught her breath, Jude reached up again to get a better look. Under the misty light cast by the street lamps, she could see them. Pigs! Hundreds of them – or at least that's what it looked like – crammed in so tight they could barely move, bumping against one other, trying to gain breathing room, some of them squealing in pain as they were stepped on or shoved against the side of the truck. It looked like something in a horror movie. What were so many pigs doing in there? She stared and stared, finally understanding that this was the last horrible night of these poor creatures lives. Shaken, she lowered herself and padded back to Eve's car. Sleep never came again, not with the sounds of the distressed pigs continuing until the first light of dawn. Jude was still keeping vigil when the truck roared to life and headed off to a place she could not have ever imagined.

Over the next several years, she struggled to find a place for herself, to make sense of a world that treated animals so badly. She handed out leaflets and joined some protests, but never seemed to find a home until she met Gordon. Ten years her senior and an idealistic, yet strong-willed organizer, he had just started The Kinship and was looking for investigators. He became mentor, friend, lover for a time, and the only person she trusted completely.

From the edge of the bed in the hotel room, she told him, "Thanks, Gordon, I'm all right. But I'd like to understand what happened, and I'd sure like to find that video."

After a long silence he said, "So would I."

CHAPTER 4

Emmet pulled into his new parking space near the office entrance, one of the spaces reserved for floor supervisors. Still dark at five thirty in the morning, the lot behind him was filling rapidly as the day shift filed in. Someone had left their lights on and he could see a parade of dull-eyed, slack-faced workers passing through the beams. He walked through the same employee entrance he had used for seven years, but this time breezed past the line of men and women waiting to pick up their blue coveralls and equipment for the day. Eyes and throats were starting to burn, a reaction to the chlorine used to clean the gloves, boots, and knives. A few of the men nodded to Emmet. He knew a handful by name, most by sight, but there were always new faces.

Grabbing a yellow hard hat and a uniform, he went down the corridor to the men's locker room. Metal doors clanged as the workers hung their coats and replaced their leather Wolverine lace-ups with thick-soled rubber boots. Emmet acknowledged the two men next to him. He liked Joe Lovato well enough, the youngest of the two and a new dad. But Tim Vernon was scary strange. Underneath his ever-present Bulls City Burger cap, he wore his long hair in a greasy braid that went to the middle of his back. He was rangy and skittish and often had the look of someone listening to a voice in his head that was not his own.

Lovato was all over Vernon's case after what had happened yesterday. He pointed to the bandage on Vernon's hand and asked, "They give you a rabies shot for that?"

"Nope. They jist gimme pills." Vernon scowled back.

"I still say that's one of the most hilarious things I ever seen. The look on your face," laughed Lovato, remembering. At the end of the shift, Vernon had reached into the bottom of his locker and been bitten by a rat. They were all over the plant.

"Yer a twat, you know that?" spat back Vernon, not in the least bit amused. "Where you are, you're probably gonna get infected with MRSA."

Lovato backed off; he knew that Vernon was easily provoked and carried a hunting knife strapped to his thigh. But in a boisterous mood and not ready for the walk to the evisceration area, he tried to keep the conversation going with Emmet. "How'd you get that?" he asked him, indicating his scar.

"Fillin' in for the sticker one day," replied Emmet as pulled on his boots. "Big boar comes rolling down the chain kicking and hollering. I thought I stuck him pretty good, but when I turn around to do the next one, he kicks me from behind. Whapp! He smacks my knife arm, which shoots up and I slice my own head. There was more of my blood on the floor than his."

"How many stitches?" This was an important figure for comparison purposes.

"Twenty-seven."

Vernon, who had been brooding in front of his locker, broke

in. "I can beat that." He pulled up his shirt to reveal a jagged, red line along his back. "Forty-two," he announced proudly. "Hog falls off the chain and starts running around the floor. We're try-ing to kill the sonofabitch any way we can. I finally get the sucker down and whiles I'm zapping it, the shackle wheel jumps off the chain and rakes me good."

"That's nothing," exclaimed Lovato. He pushed up the sleeve on his flannel shirt and showed off an ugly puckered scar that ran the length of his inner arm. "Almost had my arm tore off."

Vernon frowned, fearing this kid would beat him in the scar department. "Hog did that?"

"Nah, installing a car seat for the baby." Lovato let out a guffaw and Vernon, feeling duped somehow, snatched up his things and moved down the row.

With the men still filing in, Emmet decided he had time for a cup of coffee. He donned his hard hat and clattered up the grat-ed catwalk that led to the offices on the second floor. There he ran into Patrick LaBrie, the chief on-site inspector from the U.S. Department of Agriculture, who was waiting for a fresh batch to brew.

"Hey, Chapel, you look good in yellow. Probably matches your liver," crowed LaBrie, who was wearing the red hard hat of a USDA inspector. The workers all wore white or gray helmets, operations managers yellow, and USDA personnel red – it made them easier to spot when they came onto the floor.

Emmet wasn't in much of a mood to banter. He reached past LaBrie and pulled the glass coffee pot out of its mooring before it had finished dripping, letting the brown liquid flow onto the hot plate where it sizzled and sloshed down the sides. He poured himself half a cup and put it back.

"Good morning to you, too," said LaBrie, affronted. It hadn't occurred to him that Emmet might still be feeling raw after his friend's death. But everything about LaBrie was dense, not just his social skills. He had thick lips, a wide nose, a massive head of hair. The lenses of his black-framed glasses were so thick, Emmet used to wonder how close he had to put his face when doing his job – inspecting the hogs' heads, carcasses, and organs for signs of disease or contaminants.

Finally it dawned on LaBrie and he said, "Terrible thing about Frank."

Emmet nodded. "Yeah." The sound of the machinery cranking to life precluded further comment. Between the hammering of the compressors and shriek of the lines, it became impossible to hear each other speak. "Chain's startin'," said Emmet loudly.

"See you around," yelled LaBrie back, slapping his red helmet onto his big head.

Emmet began outside and headed around to the back of the plant. A breeze from the west brought with it notice that the trucks were waiting – the rotten egg smell of sulfur mixed with the sharp tang of ammonia from the pig manure. The sounds of snorting, squealing hogs grew louder.

There was a new driver Emmet didn't recognize helping to unload the last of the stragglers from a forty-footer. His face was red with frustration because some of the sows wouldn't budge from the truck, most likely because they couldn't walk. One had a huge abscess on her foot, another looked like it had a broken front leg and was barely able to drag herself a few feet. But they were in better shape than the one that was splayed on the truck bed near the cab – probably dead. The driver gripped a heavy plastic paddle in his elbow-length glove and smacked the sows repeatedly to get them moving. Frightened and confused, they staggered one way then another, crashing into each other and the walls of the truck, anywhere but down the ramp.

"Goddamn it!" screamed the man in pain after one of them ran into his knee. In his fury, he pulled a three-foot metal pipe from the wall of the truck and struck the offending animal on the back. Desperate to escape him, she scrambled down the ramp into the lairage pen with the others. Cursing, hollering and pummeling the pigs on any body part he could reach, the man finally got all the live ones out. Then he turned his attention to the dead pig and fastened a chain around her neck, preparing to drag her.

A skinny wise-ass nicknamed Crank, tagged for both his regular use of uppers and his quick temper, was watching along with his white co-worker on the lairage crew. They were enjoying the show. Every time one of the pigs escaped the trucker, they hooted and laughed, infuriating the man even further.

But Emmet was now a yellow hat. "C'mon! Let's get to work," he yelled.

Crank pushed back with a big grin on his face. "Shit, Chapel's management now. A supah-visah! Hey, how's the little girls' room on the second floor? Nice 'n pretty?"

"You'll never find out, asshole," said Emmet.

Crank thumped his chest and crowed, "I love the smell of pig shit in the morning!" He looked around to see if anyone appreciated his bravado, but many of the guys out here were Latino and if they understood, they didn't show it. They kept their heads down and went about their business.

"Get over here, Crank," yelled Emmet. He was inspecting the nearest pen, lot twenty-seven, packed tight with the sows just unloaded. They were in bad shape. Some were just skin and bones, the spines protruding from their backs like jagged saws with huge teeth; many had wounds that had abscessed, ears torn, and hacking coughs that suggested pneumonia. "Where're these hogs from?"

The young man shrugged, then called out the question to the trucker. The answer came back and Emmet shook his head in frustration. "I thought we weren't taking any more pigs from Heritage. They treat their animals like crap. Look at that." He pointed to a sow that had collapsed by the railing and was being trampled by the others in the overcrowded pen. Truth was, Heritage Farm wasn't even the worst of them, and Emmet had seen thousands of sick and crippled pigs come down the line. But now he felt more of a responsibility.

"Don't worry, we'll get it down the chute," reassured Crank, stepping over to kick the downed sow, who had only the strength to grunt.

"It shouldn't *go* down the goddamn chute until it's been looked at. Could be infected," exclaimed Emmet. "Where's Cimino?"

Every slaughterhouse was required to have an on-site veterinarian from the USDA in addition to the meat inspectors, and it was the vet's job to monitor the animals for signs of disease that might make them unsuitable for slaughter.

"He hasn't gotten out here yet," said Crank.

Emmet knew it was a waste of time, but he pulled out his handheld radio to page Lawrence Cimino. The vet should have already been out to look, but these days he took his time. To Emmet's thinking, Cimino was a lazy, self-satisfied old fart who didn't care about anything or anyone but himself. On the surface he came across as a kindly country doctor with tufts of gray hair on either side of his balding pate, but he was soulless at his core. The vet was sixty-three and retiring in less than a year; all he wanted was to finish out the job without incident and collect his pension.

When he didn't get any response on the second try, Emmet pocketed his radio. The crew was already corralling hogs into the drive alley, the passageway from the pens to the single-file chute that led to the stun area. The wild-eyed pigs didn't want to go. They balked at the dark tunnel and at the distressed squealing of the others around them. Several struggled to walk. This was a load of breeding sows who had been confined in metal crates their entire lives; their legs just weren't strong enough to walk the hundred feet down the chute. Some of them outright refused – they could smell death up ahead. It took five men with paddles to move them forward.

"All right. Let's go, let's go!" shouted Emmet, turning away. The chain was up and running, more trucks were waiting to unload, and he was worried that the line had already gotten off to a slow start.

CHAPTER 5

Jude knocked on the door of Frank Marino's house, a pre-fab ranch hardly bigger than a doublewide trailer. Black mold dotted the aluminum siding, but a power washer had been set up to attack the problem and the surrounding shrubs and flower beds looked carefully tended. Jude straightened her light winter jacket and smoothed back wisps of flyaway hair to look more presentable.

A tall woman with an overbite, wearing cherry-red lipstick and matching nail polish opened the door. Jude had seen her at the funeral.

"I'm sorry" said Jude. "I didn't realize Mrs. Marino had company." She turned to leave, but the woman stopped her.

"No, come on in," she said cheerily and led Jude back to a small kitchen where Verna Marino and an older woman sat at a table covered with Corningware casseroles and tinfoil-covered cookies and pies. More condolence food was heaped on the counters.

Verna looked up when Jude entered and though they had never met or spoken, there seemed to be a glint of recognition in her eyes. Perhaps it was just kindness, thought Jude, so as not to make her feel like an interloper in front of the ladies who had obviously come by to pay their respects.

"Mrs. Marino, my name's Jude Brannock," she introduced herself.

Without skipping a beat, Verna introduced Oma Burney, the older woman, and Patty Warshauer, who had let Jude in. They were both from her church, she explained.

"I don't want to interrupt," said Jude. "I can come back another time."

Rising from her chair, Oma Burney waved her off. "I have to go and take care of some things," she said smoothly. There was a momentary hitch when it became apparent that Patty Warshauer was too curious about Jude to follow her lead, but Burney took care of that herself. "Come on, Patricia. I want to show you the fabric I got on sale." Verna walked them both to the door, thanking them for their kindness and reminding them of their Bible study meeting later in the week.

When she returned, Verna stood in the doorway. One could tell that she struggled with her weight and there was a guardedness in the way she carried herself, perhaps a result of being married to a man whose fierce honesty so often created turbulence. "I saw you at the cemetery. You should have come to the house afterwards," she said to Jude kindly. "Did you know Frank?"

"I spoke to him a few times on the phone," said Jude.

"Would you like some coffee?"

"That would be nice, thank you." Jude was grateful that Verna was trying to put her at ease. She wished she had the kind of people skills that she admired in others, but for her that kind of fluency came only around animals, who were far more predictable.

After Verna brought coffee in a cup and saucer, she settled across from Jude, who got right to the point. "I work for an organization called The Kinship," she said. "Your husband contacted us about two weeks ago to report what he felt were ongoing abuses to the pigs at D&M Processing."

Verna's inviting smile remained in place, but her face seemed to have frozen into a more intractable expression.

"You're aware of what he did at the plant?" asked Jude.

"Of course, I used to work there myself," said Verna.

"What did you do?"

"I worked on the cut floor."

"Doing what?"

"Trimming shoulders." Verna mimed three swift cutting motions with her right hand, each one with her wrist at a different angle. "I did *that* for seven hours a day, six days a week, for five years."

"Why did you leave?"

Verna rubbed her wrist. "I developed tendonitis and had to stop."

Jude nodded in understanding.

"I can't actually do much with my right hand anymore," continued Verna. "Even gardening for a few minutes, it acts up."

"And your husband was on the kill floor?" asked Jude, more comfortable now in her role as investigator.

"He worked different jobs. They rotate them around."

"He told me that, among other things, animals at the plant are being beaten and kicked, sometimes dragged along the ground by their legs or necks. He filmed it."

"He what?" Verna's eyes darkened.

"You didn't know?" asked Jude. "Yes, he contacted our organization and told us that he had a lot of footage. He was going to turn it over to us. That's the reason I came to Bragg Falls. I was supposed to meet him."

Verna paled, then looked away and rubbed her temples, perhaps, thought Jude, trying to erase the idea of her husband's secretiveness.

"I guess he didn't tell you."

Verna shook her head adamantly. "No, he never said anything to me."

Feeling as though she had stumbled into a marital secret, Jude wasn't sure what to say except, "I'm so sorry about what happened."

"Frank got hurt on the job last year – his back," said Verna. "He was in quite a bit of pain. The doctor prescribed something and it seemed to help, but I had no idea that he was taking so many."

Jude took Verna's honesty as an opening and asked, "He died of an overdose of painkillers? They can be deceptively powerful, I suppose."

"I'm sure he knew that, but..." the new widow's eyes filled with anguish, "he was under a lot of stress this last year, between his back and the death of his mother and us trying to make it on one paycheck. Oh Lord, I wish I'd gotten through to him that night." As if Jude might blame her, she added defensively, "I tried to call him twice, but he didn't pick up or maybe his phone had run out of battery again. He ... didn't complain very often, but I think his back was getting worse. And now you tell me about him filming. How in the world could he get a camera in there? If they found out, they would've fired him. I'm only pulling in worker's comp and we got our daughter ..." she trailed off.

Jude stayed silent as Verna stared out the kitchen window at an empty, swaying clothesline. Finally, she continued, "You know, pigs are not bad creatures, they're playful and real smart. Before here, we were at one of the hog farms. The sows, you know ... you try to drive one of 'em into a tiny crate, she'll fight you. Make no mistake, they know what's going on. If one of them escapes from its crate when you're not around, she just might go down the whole row and unlatch the others, too. Oh yeah, they'll do that. Maybe that makes them more compassionate than us." Anger tightened the corners of her mouth. "In my church, our pastor says that God's grace is everywhere. But I can tell you God's grace is not in that slaughterhouse. Not there."

Verna seemed far away and Jude was trying to think of a way to bring her back when someone knocked on the front door. It was a uniformed officer. He had on the gray shirt and navy tie of the County Sheriff's office and carried a leather satchel. His neatly-combed hair and mustache were mostly white, and he wore the practiced expression of a man who was used to delivering bad news.

"May I come in, Mrs. Marino?" he asked respectfully, although he was already stepping inside.

"It's not Sophie, is it?" breathed Verna fearfully. Her daughter was supposed to be in school.

"No, it's not. I'm sure she's fine."

"What is it, Sheriff?"

He cast a questioning glance at Jude from the corner of his eye, and Verna quickly caught it.

"Sheriff Ward, this is Jude..."

"Brannock," Jude finished for her.

"Maybe we should talk in private," suggested Ward to Verna.

But his unannounced presence at her doorstep augured more grief and fearful of bearing it alone, she said staunchly, "You can speak in front of her."

Ward capitulated. "First, let me say how sorry I am about Frank. He was a fine man, Mrs. Marino." He cleared his throat uncomfortably. "I'm afraid that with any unnatural death, we have to investigate. And ... uh ... we found something in his car."

Frank's body had been discovered on Friday night, his car parked off a dirt road by an old country store, long abandoned and boarded up. The deputy who found him had been making routine rounds at three in the morning, spotted the car, and thinking it was kids doing things kids oughtn't to be doing checked it out. The car was locked, Frank slumped over the wheel. The deputy banged on the window and when he got no response, took a crowbar to the door. The initial findings from the County Medical Examiner were respiratory failure due to "mixed alcohol and oxycodone toxicity."

"Was Frank getting his painkillers from his doctor?" asked Ward, shifting gears.

"Yes. Dr. Shepard."

"And do you know if he was getting the prescription filled locally?"

"I suppose, why."

"Would you happen to have his medication here?"

Verna was beginning to bristle with impatience. "What are you getting at?"

"Well, we found an empty pill bottle in his car. It wasn't from Dr. Shepard and it wasn't from a pharmacy around here. It was from a place called PharmaRX. You ever heard of it?"

"No, but what does that have to with his death?"

"The bottle we found listed the dose at 30 milligram strength and we know that Dr. Shepard was prescribing the 15 milligram ones. Frank might have been taking extra pills. We also found this in the car," he said, bringing out a laptop computer from his satchel.

"That's Frank's," exclaimed Verna, wide-eyed.

Ward said, "I think I need to show you something."

They went into the kitchen, where Ward sat at the table, adjusting his leather gun belt to fit the back of the chair. "It looks like he did make a purchase from PharmaRX a couple of weeks ago," he said, pointing to the screen. Then he clicked on a box at the top of the screen and pulled up a history of sites visited by the user. "These are all websites and chat rooms that he visited recently," he said. There was a list of a dozen links, and as Ward scrolled through, they described sites that discussed oxycodone overdosing. Ward landed on the last – an interactive page where people could post questions and get answers from others out in cyberspace. At the top of the page was the written inquiry: *What is a lethal dose of oxycodone in opiate tolerant people?*

The normally rich color drained completely from Verna's face. Her mouth moved silently almost in prayer before she finally was able to manage, "Are you telling me that my husband committed suicide?"

Ward didn't respond directly. Frank's intent seemed clear.

CHAPTER 6

The corporate headquarters of Marshfield Industries had the feel of a well-endowed southern college. Every mahogany arch and cream-colored cornice was meticulously designed, the oriental rugs on the richly varnished floors hand picked. But for all the old-school charm, modernity was not lacking. When Ned Bannerman, back from his regional tour of Marshfield's meat packing plants, rang the buzzer of an unmarked door on the second floor, his image was captured from several angles by hidden, state-of-the-art security cameras. He had to wait until he was cleared before the door clicked open.

A guard at the desk directed him around the corner to another closed door. This one was marked with a gold plaque: Richard Hillman, Director, OSM. When Bannerman entered, Hillman was sitting at his desk. He was in his fifties and looked like an army man who had let himself go. His suit jacket hung open to reveal a sizeable paunch and the broken blood vessels across his nose and cheeks marked him as a man who liked his whiskey. But his eyes were sharp, as were his knife-edged planning skills. One of the few people who reported directly to Seldon Marshfield, his was the Office of Systems Management – a nebulous title for Marshfield's corporate damage control.

"Have a seat," said Hillman, waving to a burgundy leather chair opposite the desk.

"How's your short game these days?" asked Bannerman. The regional VP usually carried himself with the confidence that would be expected of a thirty-nine-year-old MBA who had been instrumental in putting the company back into the black after the economic slump. But in Hillman's unaccommodating presence he wasn't quite as sure of himself. Trying to break the ice, he chuckled, "A funny story ... I was on the ninth hole over at Brier Creek–"

"Save it for the board, Ned," interrupted Hillman brusquely. "Let's talk about this D&M video fiasco. Go over for me again how it all started."

Bannerman was under no illusion that the OSM Director wasn't already fully aware of the circumstances and would further choreograph whatever moves were necessary, but he knew that Hillman liked to make people – even his own people – repeat their stories so he could look for inconsistencies.

Clearing his throat, Bannerman began, "Well, one of the employees reported seeing a co-worker around the pens when he wasn't supposed to be there and it looked suspicious. That same worker had a history of sending out complaints, so the plant manager Bob Warshauer was worried he might have brought in a camera. He instituted bag searches, but nothing turned up. Somehow, Bob figured out that this guy had made a video inside."

"You're aware, Ned, that *this guy,* Frank Marino, recorded the conversation between you and Warshauer. We got it off Marino's computer and I've listened to it. What the hell were you thinking?"

Flushing deeply, Bannerman said, "I don't understand how it could have happened. We were behind closed doors, no one could hear us."

"Marino was in the crawl space below the building."

"What was he doing down there?"

"He was putting out rat poison, and apparently air ducts from the office carried your message from Seldon loud and clear right onto his camcorder."

"Oh, Jesus." Bannerman ran a hand over his face. "I had no idea, I swear. I ... I was there on Seldon's behalf–"

Hillman waved off any further explanation and continued, "Moreover, we learned that Marino planned to turn over the recording to a woman from an animal rights organization who, as I understand it, is on her way to Bragg Falls, or possibly already there."

A sheen of sweat broke out on Bannerman's forehead and upper lip. The situation was getting worse by the minute. "How ... how did you find out about the recording?"

"Bob Warshauer called me directly and I had Marino's phone calls monitored."

As if that was the most reasonable thing to do, Bannerman nodded and asked, "What's going to happen?" He tried to keep the anxiety out of his voice, but it was damn difficult, knowing that Hillman enjoyed taking him down a notch.

"Oh, I didn't tell you?" asked Hillman innocently. "Marino turned over the video, and his camera, too."

"Before the animal rights people got it?"

"Yes, Ned, we believe so. And just so you know, her name is Jude Brannock. I haven't had any dealings with her, although I know her boss Gordon Silverman. He's tenacious as hell, and these activists are a nagging problem right now. Still, their resources are

minimal, so if Brannock doesn't get any cooperation or information, she'll have to pack up and go home. It's imperative that no
one at the plant talk to her. I'll deal with Bob Warshauer on that."

The sense of reprieve that washed over Bannerman almost
made him lightheaded, but he did manage to ask, "What about
Frank Marino?"

"Ah, yes," Hillman heaved a dispirited sigh. "My heart goes
out to his family. Apparently there was a suicide. Such a tough,
tough thing to deal with. You never know what's in a man's mind.
Not really."

Bannerman's relief was cut short. *Suicide?* Shifting in his seat,
he felt his trousers stick to leather. He didn't know what to make
of this information, but there was no way he was going to inquire.
He was dangling off a ledge and Hillman would decide whether
he'd get pulled up or pushed off.

Abruptly, Hillman ended the meeting. "You hear anything,
keep me posted."

A moment after Bannerman left, a man stepped into the office
through a side door. There was an almost boyish look about him. He
had a taut, muscled body and sandy brown hair parted on the side
so that a lock almost always fell disarmingly over his brow. Today he
was dressed in a pair of four-hundred-dollar Cucinelli chinos, tas-
seled loafers costing double that, and a black t-shirt from The GAP.

"I suppose he'll figure it out," remarked Hillman.

Bloom shrugged.

"You're right, it doesn't matter," said Hillman. "Bannerman's
greedy. He plans to move up from regional to sit at Seldon's right
hand. I'm still concerned about the recording, though. Do you
believe Marino, that he didn't make a copy?"

"After I made a single copy for you, I did everything we discussed. Relevant files were deleted from his computer, and others

were added. PharmaRX records will show the order put on Marino's credit card. There won't be any problems. Did Marino make himself a duplicate? I didn't know the man, but he seemed ready to put everything behind him for the sake of his family."

Hillman relied on Bloom's uncanny ability to read weakness, which is why he went with the hired gun's assurance that in a stressful situation Frank Marino would do almost anything to have a drink. In this instance, a drink that had been doctored while Frank was in the Lazy Cat. Nevertheless, Hillman rubbed a nervous hand across his desk, as though he were wiping away a film of dust. "If there is a copy down there we cannot let Brannock or anyone else get their hands on it. Even without Marino, if it got turned over to the media ... I don't even want to think about it. Because we're not going to let that happen. Stick around Bragg Falls for now," he instructed. "Keep tabs on the situation, but low profile, yes?"

Bloom didn't answer, busy removing a speck of lint from his trousers. His fastidiousness came off as preening, but Hillman was unfazed by the overt narcissism; it was part of what made him as good as he was. Besides, he had only to glance at the missing chunk of Bloom's left pinky finger to remind them both that mistakes could be made.

CHAPTER 7

Jude watched as Finn galloped unevenly along the path, his right hind paw barely grazing the ground. His limp was a life-long condition, but it had not touched his spirit. She had rescued him as a puppy when he couldn't have been more than four or five weeks old. That winter in Vermont was cold and the puppy mill owner, a French Canadian, had been keeping at least two dozen females in wire cages outside in unheated sheds. Many were sick and malnourished, the worst of them the mixed breeds whose pups wouldn't be worth much. Boiling with fury, Jude roared down the country roads to track down the local sheriff and drag him back out to arrest the owner while she made arrangements with a local shelter to take the dogs. During the heated argument between the owner and the sheriff, Jude found the pup behind the sheds in a rusty, metal cage with a broken sign on it that read "Fin" – the French word for finished. Ended. Indeed, from the feed scale next to the crate, she suspected the owner was selling dead dogs by the pound, probably to a rendering plant nearby. Her dog wasn't finished, however. His hind leg was mangled, but he was still struggling to escape the cage from under the weight of a pile of dead puppies. She picked him up, warmed him underneath her coat, and called him Finn. He would do anything for her.

The early afternoon light filtered through the honey-colored and russet leaves above their heads. They both needed some exercise and there were no signs at the state park telling her that dogs had to be leashed. So Jude unclipped his leash at the head of a trail marked by splotches of yellow paint on the trees. Finn bounded in and out of the woods, staying well ahead of her, and she followed as the trail began to climb. The higher they went, the rockier and more uneven the path became, but it was well-marked and Jude was not worried about getting back.

She breathed in the autumn air, feeling the muscles in her legs work and thinking about Frank Marino. Why was he despondent? It was disturbing to imagine that it had something to do with contacting The Kinship. But how could she have known that he was suicidal? *The man worked at a slaughterhouse for God's sake,* she thought, *it wouldn't be the first time the job drove someone out of his mind.*

At one point, Jude found herself trudging along the side of a ridge that sloped steeply off to her right until finally the ground flattened and opened up to a scenic overlook. The view was breathtaking – rolling hills covered with deciduous trees displaying their fall colors that became muted in a haze of distant blue. Jude bent over and put her hands on her knees to catch her breath, staring with wonder at the vista. She almost didn't notice the girl sitting with her back against a tree and reaching out her hand to scratch Finn under the chin.

The girl jumped up. "Oh, sorry," she said, as if she'd been caught doing something wrong. "Is it okay to pet your dog?" She looked to be in her mid-teens and an unlikely combination of punk rocker and athlete. Her nose was pierced with a silver stud, her right ear adorned with a row of hooped earrings, and her hair cropped in an I-don't-care-what-I-look-like mane with ragged bangs that now lay plastered in wet strips against her brow. Noting her worn Nikes and an empty water bottle, Jude guessed she'd been doing some serious running.

"It looks like you two have already gotten to know each other," said Jude.

The girl knelt down and stroked the fur along Finn's back. "He's got beautiful eyes," she said.

"Doesn't he?"

"What's his name?"

"Finn."

"Finn," she repeated reverently. "What kind of dog is he?"

"I don't really know, he's a mix. I'm guessing he was supposed to be a Rottweiler, but his mom had other plans or maybe the breeder didn't know a Rottie from a Sheepdog, which is why he didn't end up in a pet store."

"I wanted to have a dog, but my folks wouldn't let me. Both my parents work and they said no one would be home to take care of it."

"What's your name?"

"Caroline."

"Hi, I'm Jude." She recognized Caroline as one of the two girls that caught her attention at the gravesite. "You must be Sophie's friend. I'm sorry about her father."

"How do you know that?"

"I was at the cemetery."

"I didn't see you there."

"I kept my distance. Frank and I were just acquaintances. You knew him pretty well?"

"Yeah, I mean Sophie and I have been best friends since ... I don't know ... second grade? He was a really good dad."

"Tough thing to lose your father at such a young age."

"She was at my house when she found out. Her mom came and got her. It was pretty bad."

Jude let the girl sift through the memory of that moment before asking gently, "Where is Sophie now?"

"Oh, she's at school."

"And you're not?" A questioning smile played on Jude's lips.

Caroline responded with a disinterested shrug, although she couldn't entirely hide the color that came into her cheeks. "School is a waste of time," she complained, waving in the general direction behind her.

"I used to feel like that," said Jude, who wisely held back a lecture about how wrong she was. "Are you a runner?"

Walking over to the protective wooden railing at the cliff's edge, Caroline threw over her shoulder, "Why all the questions?"

"You don't have to answer, but I just figured any friend of Finn is a friend of mine," said Jude, coming up to join her.

"I used to be on the track team," Caroline offered, "but it was so pointless I quit. I like to run, though."

"Don't tell me you *ran* all the way up here."

"Most of the way. Some of it I have to walk."

"You must be in great shape. How come you quit the team?"

"You have to follow their incredibly stupid training methods or they go ballistic," Caroline bemoaned. "Story of my life. School, home, every time I turn around, I'm breaking some rule or other."

"I know a little about that," confessed Jude.

"My dad is a jerk and he's getting worse all the time. Just about everything I do sets him off. He hates the way I look, he hates my boyfriend. He just wants me to be this happy, dimwitted cheerleader – his little cookie-cutter girl. He was best friends with Frank, did you know that?"

"No, I didn't." Jude pictured the lone man standing by Frank's gravesite. "Does your father work at D&M as well?" When Caroline nodded, she added, "Hard way to make a living."

"Nobody asked him to. I sure didn't. He could have been a carpenter or plumber or something, but we had to stay in this pathetic town so he could work at a *slaughterhouse.*"

"You don't approve?"

Caroline shook her head impatiently at the question and said, "When he comes home he stinks to high heaven. Just like this whole town. I hate it. Everyone here is like incredibly dumb and the place smells like manure year round."

Gazing out at the majestic view, Jude took a deep breath. "Not up here," she said.

"That's why this is my favorite place. It's clean and pure, you know? I feel ... safe up here. Doesn't smell like pig shit."

Jude laughed, "Yeah, you gotta give yourself a break every once in a while." She looked over hoping to catch a smile from the girl and was surprised to see her so morose. It didn't seem natural for a teenager.

Caroline reached into the pocket of her hoodie for her cell phone. "I have to go," she said when she saw the time on the screen. "I have a shrink appointment. Because I'm such a troublemaker and so *crazy!*" Finn had come up between them and put his head into Caroline's outstretched hand.

"He really likes you," said Jude, genuinely impressed.

"So long, Finn. I hope to see you again." Caroline bent down to nuzzle the top of his head. Then without another word she began her long-legged jog back down the trail.

Underneath Caroline's defiance was a heartache that reminded Jude of herself at that age. She'd been angry too, but learned quickly that her protests were no match for the crusted remains the state handed out to kids like her. Fairness was just a concept, like algebra. It had nothing to do with the living, breathing, hungering realities of every day life. Jude stared after Caroline until she disappeared in the trees and wondered what was troubling the girl so.

CHAPTER 8

"This is great, just great," said Emmet, his patience at an end. "We both leave work to get here and she can't even show up on time."

"Maybe one of her teachers kept her after class," Alice suggested limply.

In lieu of offering an opinion, Dr. Ohler cleared his throat and said, "We could use this time to talk about any concerns that you have regarding Caroline." Barry Ohler, a psychologist, was an unimaginative but kind man with a pinched face and wire-framed glasses. The Chapels had been steered to him by Caroline's school counselor, and this was to have been their first meeting as a family.

"Well, my first *concern* is that she's wasting our time and probably enjoying it," said Emmet disgustedly.

"She certainly is making a statement," Ohler remarked.

"Yeah, she makes a lot of those," said Emmet.

"Emmet, please," Alice interjected. "We're here to help Caroline." She turned her attention to Ohler. "You've met with her now a few times. And you talked to her regular doctor, right? There's nothing physically wrong with her. So what do you think this whole end of the world thing is about? And her obsession with death?"

"I'm telling you, it's for effect," Emmet broke in irritably. "To get attention. I mean, look at us – we interrupt our day, risk our jobs to come here, and she's got everyone talking about *Caroline.*"

"Why do you have to be so hard on her?" his wife challenged.

"I'm only as hard as she forces me to be," he defended. "She's always got some gripe to act out at home, and there's absolutely no reason for it – she's got everything a girl could want."

"She's hurting, Emmet. Can't you see that?"

Her husband looked away and fixed his eyes on the doctor's desk where he saw a framed photograph of two smiling teenagers. Their happy faces flooded him with renewed anger at his daughter for her crazy obsession, made more perverse by the real death of his friend.

The doctor cleared his throat again, this time to diffuse the tension between husband and wife. "In a way, you're both right," he said. "Her rebellion and shutting you out – some of that is normal adolescent behavior. But I think that her preoccupation with death is a sign that she's depressed. It's not uncommon. Often the only way teens can express their feelings is by saying that they hate themselves or they hate you. But in a way, she's calling out to you, saying, 'Hey, I'm so unhappy that I fear death.'"

Alice gripped the sides of her chair and said, "But I don't think she *fears* it, Dr. Ohler. I think she almost ... welcomes it."

"According to her, it's *inevitable*," corrected Emmet harshly.

"Well, she wouldn't be wrong there," Ohler offered with a weak laugh.

Alice was not amused. "Not at age sixteen!"

"No, of course not." The doctor righted himself, taking off

his glasses and cleaning them. "Um ... when did you notice the change in her behavior?"

"There seemed to be a big change about a month ago," replied Alice.

"Did anything happen in school that you're aware of?"

"No, in fact she was doing fairly well in her classes, she had friends, she was running track. And then out of the blue, she gets her nose pierced without our permission, she chops off her hair–"

Emmet interrupted, "Dresses like a hooker and starts up with that kid." When Ohler raised his eyebrows, he explained, "The boyfriend. I think there's something wrong with him. Wears only black and smokes dope."

"She hardly says a word to us anymore," continued Alice. "I thought maybe it was just adolescent behavior, but then I found the clippings in her room, and that's when we called the school counselor."

"The clippings ... you mean obituaries?" confirmed Ohler.

Alice leaned forward and said, "Not only is she cutting out obituaries from the newspapers, but she writes her own – about herself."

"And this apocalypse nonsense," Emmet added.

"Has she ever said anything about *how* she thinks she's going to die?" asked Ohler.

"I overheard her talking to her friend Sophie on the phone, telling her something ridiculous about her trip to Rome and that it might happen there."

"Oh, is she going to Rome?" asked the doctor.

"Of course not," said Emmet, finding the prospect absurd. "But she's taking Italian at school, so she thinks it's very romantic to talk about Italy."

"What has she said to you?" Alice asked the doctor.

"I can't tell you that, it would be a breach of confidentiality.

I can tell you, however, that she hasn't been very forthcoming. But that's not unusual," he added quickly, "and we're working on building trust."

"How long is that going to take?" asked Emmet.

"Hard to say."

"Oh, for Christ's sake." Emmet threw himself back in his chair in frustration.

"What can we do?" pleaded Alice.

"Listen to her when she's willing to talk to you. Try not to denigrate her feelings, just listen. I know her doctor prescribed medication, so make sure she's taking that."

With anxiety tightening her voice to the cracking point, Alice asked, "Dr. Ohler, is … is Caroline at risk for suicide? I mean, just to prove to us she's right?"

"Don't be so dramatic, mother," said Caroline from the door. She had changed back into her school clothes, such as they were, not wanting to give away to her parents that she was running. She strode in and flounced onto a chair next to her mom.

"You're late," announced Emmet.

No one backed him up; instead Ohler gave her a warm smile. "Hi, Caroline. Your folks and I were just talking. They're very concerned that you might be depressed. Is there anything you'd like to talk about?"

"Yeah, the meds are giving me diarrhea. And considering I may not have long to live, I don't think that's fair."

"Give it a little time, Caroline," advised Ohler. "It takes a while for the medication to work and your body to get acclimated."

"I looked it up on line, and I guess I should tell you if I get pregnant, right? Because of the harm to the fetus."

"Oh Caroline, just cut it out," snapped her father.

"Well, it's true. And I also think we have to acknowledge that antidepressants in teens can actually *lead* to suicide," she lectured. "So I guess we'd better keep a closer eye on me ... if that's even possible."

"Are you upset about being grounded?" asked Dr. Ohler sympathetically.

"Are you kidding? It's my heart's desire to be sixteen and imprisoned in a tiny house with my parents and my little brother. I can't drive, I can't do anything."

"We're supposed to let you behind the wheel while you're fixated on death? I don't think so," rebuked Emmet.

"Well, trapping me in this fucking nowhere town is not going to make it go away!"

"Watch yourself," growled her father.

Caroline shot Dr. Ohler a look that begged for agreement on how difficult her father was. But the doctor was already forming his next line of inquiry. "We're trying to understand what makes you feel like death is around the corner for you."

Her father had one leg crossed over the other showing the bottom of his work boot stained with dried manure and pigs' blood. It made her want to throw up. She hated him. She hated her mother's ill-fitting Walmart uniform, the dry skin stretched over her cheekbones and the smell of the cheap strawberry-scented shampoo they both had to share. A part of her wanted to scream as loud as she could and run out the door, but every once in a while her own thoughts scared her, coming out of nowhere and sending her into a panic. So she tried to explain. "It's like ... something inside me just knows. Maybe it's my soul. Because when I think about it, my mind says I have no reason to believe I'll die. I'm not sick, I don't particularly want to die, and my mind is giving me all these other options. But I know that my mind is not always right." She struggled to find the words. "My mind makes mistakes a lot. It makes me do kind of destructive things and say dumb stuff. But the soul doesn't. It's like the soul is pure – it's the real *you*. I mean, after you're dead, that's what will exist ... it's all you really have, which is why I think my soul is telling me something I need to know."

"And your soul is telling you that you're going to die?" asked the doctor gently.

She nodded and then looked down at her hands, if only to avoid seeing her father's reproach. In fact, it wouldn't have been censure she would have seen, but sorrow, deeper and more helpless than her own.

CHAPTER 9

E arly the next morning, Jude picked up a local newspaper and brought it to the diner where she hoped to find some people from the plant willing to talk. Like everything else in town, the eatery had the feel of resignation. Despite the sign out front that promised "REAL FOOD," from the pungent aroma of grease and tobacco that met her when she pushed through the door, Jude had misgivings. Several heads turned her way to check out the stranger. The table area was barely half full, but she chose a seat at the counter next to two guys discussing a carburetor problem with a man Jude figured to be the owner. His large frame was planted behind the counter. Encircled by a stained apron, he wore lightly tinted glasses that precluded a good look at his eyes. But he was the same man pictured in the photographs thumbtacked to the back wall showing him, shotgun slung over his shoulder, proudly holding the heads of various deer, coyotes, and bobcats he had killed.

A waitress appeared and slid a worn plastic menu in front of Jude. "Coffee?" she asked.

Jude nodded. "Black, please." She didn't think there would be anything on the menu she could eat so she pushed it aside and opened the paper. Most of the news centered around the nearby city of Abbeville: early retirement for a county commissioner, a piece on rising gas prices, and weather analysis for the farmers. At the end of the crime blog there was a paragraph about Frank Marino. The Medical Examiner cited the cause of death as a toxic mix of painkillers and alcohol, concluding that the Bragg Falls man thought to have accidentally overdosed had, in fact, committed suicide. He worked at D&M Processing and was survived by his wife and daughter.

The waitress returned with a mug of weak, black coffee and asked Jude if she was ready to order.

"Just a toasted English muffin, no butter, and a glass of orange juice, thanks."

The waitress eyed her suspiciously; this was a place to eat "real food" and lots of it. And the owner, a few feet away, chimed in, "You gonna waste away, s'all you eat."

"I'm not that hungry," replied Jude.

"Well, when you git hungry, I'd all recommend the biscuits 'n gravy." He pointed to the mound of thick, beige slop on a plate belonging to the man next to Jude.

"Maybe next time," smiled Jude.

"Name's Roy Mears. You from 'round heah?" he asked.

"No, I'm from Virginia. Just visiting a friend."

"That so? Just about everyone in Bragg Falls comes through here, maybe I know her."

"Actually, it's a him." Jude pointed to the paragraph about Frank. "And unfortunately, he just died."

Mears squinted at the paper, then drew back. "Frank Marino? Oh yeah, I heard about that. Damn shame," he said, shaking his head. "What's the paper say?"

"Apparently his death has been ruled a suicide."

"Goddamn. Hey, Lenny," he tapped his spatula on the counter to get the attention of one of the men next to Jude. "You used to work over to D&M. You know a guy named Frank Marino? Guy who killed hisself."

"I thought he overdosed," said Lenny.

"Yeah, dimwit, that's how he killed hisself," guffawed Mears.

"No shit." Lenny elbowed his partner. "Jesse, you know Frank Marino?"

He thought for a moment. "Name sounds familiar. He was at D&M."

Now Jude had three of them talking. "Hard to understand, isn't it?" she prompted.

"Not that hard," scoffed Lenny. "Not if you've put in time over there."

"I guess a lot of folks around here work at the plant," said Jude.

"Sure do," Jesse said, looking around him. "But not all the right kind of folks, if you ask me."

"How so?"

Roy Mears leaned over the counter and lowered his voice to a conspiratorial mumble. "Too many Mexicans," he said from the side of his mouth, "Comin' up, takin' our jobs."

"Who else you gonna get to butcher hogs?" asked Lenny. "I worked there for six months outta high school. It's a shit awful job."

"Yeah, but the Mexicans come up here illegal, then we gotta educate their kids and pay their hospital bills."

"They spend money same's us," Lenny pointed out.

Mears threw up his hands. "Don't get me wrong, I'm willing to serve them. But I just think they should learn to talk English."

Jude tried to steer the conversation back to D&M. "I heard

some of the conditions are pretty bad at the plant. For the workers," she said.

"Lady, you have no idea," said Lenny.

"And for the animals."

"Them, too."

"For fuck's sake, they're pigs," said Mears irritably. "They jis' bacon."

"Mebbe, but they don't wanna die," Lenny protested.

"And the animals are often mishandled?" pressed Jude.

Apparently that was one question too many because the three men abruptly stopped talking. The clatter of dishes sounded in the background. Mears lowered his glasses to peer at Jude more carefully and said, "Whoa, hold a minute. What're you, some kind of animal rights person?"

She looked him square in the eye and nodded. If she'd been working undercover, she'd have made an attempt to deflect the question, but then again, if she'd been undercover she wouldn't be in here poking around.

"I've heard about you people," accused Mears, turning away to flip a couple of fried eggs on the griddle. "You're like some kind of eco-terrorist. Save th'animals and all that other crap." He pointed the spatula at her for emphasis. "We had someone like you come around a couple of years ago and try to shut D&M down."

"If they're violating the law, shouldn't they be held accountable?" Jude wasn't to be cowed.

Mears countered, "You're a good one to talk about the law. You'd blow up a building to save a goddamn rat. That's just plain terrorism and they oughta put your type in jail."

The waitress swept by, plates in hand. "Roy, how're those burgers coming?" she asked irritably. "Table two is waiting."

Mears abruptly turned his back and peeled off two frozen

beef patties to throw on the grill. They hissed, sending a cloud of grease-filled steam into the air.

"Don't mind him," Lenny said to Jude. "He gets prickly when things are slow. You gotta understand, D&M employs more'n half this town. If it goes under, this place goes under, too. Everyone is struggling to stay afloat."

His friend Jesse chimed in, "I got a cousin in Texas who runs an auto body shop. When they closed one of the local meat packing plants on account of the drought, he says business dropped off 'bout a third. People are moving out."

Jude sighed, "I understand."

She heard Roy Mears mutter *bullshit* under his breath and thought it was probably time to move on. She left her half-eaten English muffin and a tip on the counter. While she was paying her check at the cash register, a man wearing a pair of coveralls and a camouflage cap got up from one of the tables and walked out, brushing rudely, deliberately against her as she passed.

Jude had been branded. An *animal activist* was in town.

* * *

She was unlocking her car when she heard someone calling, "Miss!" Jude turned to see a young man trotting across the parking lot to catch up with her. Light brown complexioned, in his late twenties, he had a feathery goatee on his chin and shoulder-length black hair tied back in a pony tail.

"Miss," he said. "I heard you talking about Mr. Marino inside." He had a slight Latino accent, but his English carried the fluency of someone who had spent a few years in the states. "Frank was a friend."

"I'm sorry," said Jude. "You were close?"

"Not like family, but he was my boss. I wanted to come to his funeral, but I couldn't get off."

Jude introduced herself and in turn, he offered his name as Juan. She didn't think that was his real name, but didn't press it. He probably had reasons to protect himself.

"We heard about his suicide," he said.

"Yes, very sad," said Jude, and after being so soundly rebuffed in the diner, grasped at any information. "I guess he was unhappy at D&M."

"Ain't no one happy there."

"I heard he was particularly upset about how the plant is run."

"Well, he was always trying to take care of us, you know?"

"How did he do that?"

"Stood up to management."

"About what?" Jude wanted to know.

The young man looked around uneasily, wondering if anyone could see them together. "A lot of stuff," he said hurriedly. "Bad conditions for the workers and ... the animals."

Jude leaned in. "What about the animals?"

He glanced over his shoulder again. The man in the camouflage cap was loitering by the diner's entrance, watching them. "Listen, I can't talk anymore." He began to walk around the corner to the back of the diner.

Pocketing her car keys, Jude kept step beside him. "Juan, I want to learn about what's happening at D&M. It's not good for the workers there or the pigs. Could I just ask you a couple of questions?"

"No, no." He kept going.

"Please. All confidential, I'll keep your name out of it, I promise."

Leery about what *it* was, Juan picked up his pace to shake her off. But Jude sensed a possible ally.

"People are getting hurt at the plant," she pursued. "And the animals are suffering needlessly, aren't they? How can anything change if it's all brushed under the rug? Frank contacted me because he wanted to do something about it." This stopped his retreat. "That's why I came to Bragg Falls ... to find out what he knew. Listen, we don't have to meet in public and I won't mention your name. Please."

He scratched nervously at his goatee and Jude held her breath; when it came to animal abuse, many people wanted to talk. Whether they had witnessed mistreatment or been complicit, deep down they felt bad and needed to unload their burden. But just then, there was the sound of boots crunching on gravel. The man in cap and coveralls rounded the corner. He made his fingers into a gun, pointed at them and mimed pulling the trigger. Juan bolted, running past an old flatbed truck on cinderblocks, then disappearing into the tall weeds.

CHAPTER 10

Across town, Emmet stepped onto the kill floor, absorbing the one-two punch of stench and noise. The foul odor of offal, stomach contents and human sweat was smothering and the noise like claws that dug into his skull. Hooks clanked on the chain, pigs grunted and squealed, workers shouted, all of it competing with the strident whine of the overhead ventilation fans. The sounds rang in his ears long after the line shut down for the day, until the fourth or fifth beer finally quieted them so that he could watch TV. He adjusted his orange ear plugs and noted the time on his clipboard.

Tim Vernon was manning the stun station. A lot could go wrong at D&M, but more often than not, this is where it started. The hogs were driven from the chute into V-shaped restraining panels that squeezed the pigs to hold them steady. The restrainer then carried them forward until they got to Vernon, who grasped a large electrically charged device with two contacts for either side of the pig's head and a third angled to connect with its back. Emmet watched as Vernon forced the tongs down onto a sow, delivering the two hundred and fifty volts meant to send her into instant cardiac arrest. With a shudder, the sow slumped, and the restrainer deposited the animal with a wet thud onto the shackle table, where another man pulled a linked chain down from the overhead pulley system and wrapped it around one of the sow's hind feet. As the pulley chugged along, it lifted the shackled hog into a vertical position, swinging head down, ready for the sticker. The men worked with a fierce concentration; no movement could be wasted – not with a live animal coming through every seven seconds.

Next to Vernon stood a recent hire watching how the stunning was done. It was evident that this was his first time because his eyes were wide with apprehension. Whether it was due to the brutal felling of the animals in such rapid succession or the mercilessness with which Vernon did it was unclear. Emmet tapped him on the shoulder and drew him aside.

"Did you get the written instructions?" he shouted.

"Que?"

Emmet used hand gestures to indicate a book and shouted, "Instrucciones?"

"Si, si," said the man and reached into his back pocket. He pulled out a crumpled piece of paper printed with a few lines of Spanish and a diagram of where to place the tongs against the pig's head and back.

"That's all they gave you?" asked Emmet. Before he could get a reply, his attention was drawn to a nearby commotion. The man at the shackling table was screaming at Vernon, and Emmet shouldered his way forward to find out what the problem was.

"Just do your fucking job!" yelled the shackler, who was struggling to get a particularly large sow up on the chain. Only momentarily stunned, she had regained consciousness and was scrambling to get to her feet, hooves scraping and slipping on the metal table. "Get the fuck over here and hit it again!" he screamed at Vernon.

Vernon shot him the finger and put the tongs on the next one coming through. But the first jolt didn't have much effect other than to drive the sow wild; it let loose an ear-piercing squeal and bucked against the restrainer, making it almost impossible for Vernon to place the tongs for a second shot. "Fuck your mother!" he shouted at the sow as he tried to make contact anywhere he could. He fired and this time the hog dropped.

"What's going on?" Emmet bellowed.

"I don't have enough juice," Vernon yelled back, getting ready for another. "Not for these big suckers."

Damn. The USDA vet had said he'd be coming by in thirty minutes and Warshauer had probably turned the voltage down, forgetting that they had a load of sows coming in today. If the voltage was set too high, it often resulted in burst capillaries along the pig's back. Called blood-splash, they left dark patches on the meat, reducing its value. But when the hogs weren't properly stunned they became conscious again within seconds and the shacklers down the line had a fight on their hands to get them hung. For the most part, the hogs that came in were all the same size, bred to be identical and sent to slaughter at the same age. But the spent breeding sows were much larger, and wrestling with a terrified four or five-hundred pound hog was a dangerous job.

Emmet let the men at the shackling table handle the situation for the moment and trotted down the line, waving his arm in a big circle – a signal to keep getting the hogs up no matter what.

The shackler yelled at him as he went by. "Stop the fuckin' chain, will ya!"

"No can do," Emmet tossed back. He moved on quickly, knowing he'd be in this bind for years to come. Hanging a conscious, struggling hog was not only a violation, but could get someone hurt. As the man in charge, he was the only one with the authority to hit the red button. But he'd known supervisors who had gotten fired on the spot for doing that. You did not stop the chain for a couple of live hogs – not if you wanted to make it to your next pay day.

Frank's voice rang in his ears. *Get out? This doesn't get you out. It digs you in deeper.* Goddamn Frank. Always making the problems on the floor worse by fighting about it with management. They'd first met at a mandatory meeting for new workers a few years back. The USDA vet Lawrence Cimino was instructing them that kicking and gasping in a stunned hog did not mean that it was conscious – it was a reflexive movement only. Frank raised his hand. "What does it mean when a hog jumps off the table and runs across the floor?" he asked as he picked a piece of white fat off his shirt and flicked it across the room. Cimino looked over his glasses first at the spot where the fat landed and then at Frank. He said with a frosty smile. "It means someone hasn't done his job." Frank looked over at Emmet and the silent exchange between them marked a new friendship.

Thoughts of Frank only brought back his last words to Emmet. *You're not yellow hat material ... keep the line moving so corporate can squeeze us for the extra buck.* He thrust the memory aside and strode quickly down the line, careful not to slip on the blood-soaked floor. As he closed in on the sticker – the man next in line who cut the hog's carotid and jugular veins to bleed it out – he whistled through his teeth, three high-pitched, short whistles to warn him that a conscious hog might be coming his way.

"Sonofabitch," cried the sticker, wiping the sweat from his face with the sleeve of his blood stained uniform. Then he gripped his knife tight in his hand and balanced on the balls of his feet in case he had to dodge flailing legs and biting teeth in his one chance to make a good stick. Emmet paused, waiting to see what was coming down the line, but Vernon must have hit the next ones right because they were all hanging the way they should – a few of them still making reflexive paddling motions, but none bucking or squealing. He cast a quick glance at the scalding tank further on down, where the bled pigs were submerged for hair removal. For now, things seemed to be running smoothly, but he wanted to keep it that way.

Emmet threw open a steel door to an area where the ever-whirring knife sharpeners were kept along with the hoses and cleaning equipment. The control box was just inside the door, set into the wall. He reached up to open the front panel only to find a shiny new padlock affixed to the latch.

Suddenly he felt a presence behind him. Thinking it was Pat LaBrie, he turned to tell him off. But it was the plant manager.

"What are you doing?" demanded Warshauer.

Emmet took him head on. "I'm turning it up. We have a shipment of big sows coming through and Vernon doesn't have enough juice."

Warshauer shook his head. "Screw him. He came in here yesterday and tried to jack it up himself. He's a whack job. Pat LaBrie counted seven hogs with blood-splash."

"Seven out of five thousand?" challenged Emmet. "So what? It doesn't ruin the whole hog."

"Nope. That's meat I cannot sell."

"Oh, for Christ's sake, a couple of pounds?"

"Listen, you better start thinking about it in terms of ounces," replied Warshauer irritably.

"Tell that to Cimino," replied Emmet. "He's making his grand entrance, coming down to have a look in about fifteen minutes."

Warshauer practically jumped. "Shit!" He fumbled for his keys, opened the lock on the control box, and re-set the voltage. Then he turned back to Emmet and said, "Clean up and come to the office."

After stripping off his coveralls and chlorinating his boots so as not to bring pathogens into the "cold" side of the building where the eviscerated hogs were cut into sellable pieces, Emmet trotted up the metal steps to the catwalk that ran outside the offices overlooking the cut floor. Warshauer was there, patrolling the walkway, making sure that all workers were in place and doing their jobs. From his elevated position he could ascertain from the color of the helmets where the key personnel were positioned, including the red hats of the USDA inspectors.

Warshauer saw him coming. "Why is Cimino going on the floor?" he demanded. "Who complained?" Before Emmet could respond, he leaned over the railing, having spotted a couple of women below on the floor removing their aprons. "Yo, ladies, where are you going?" he called down.

One of the women, whose dark hair was piled thickly into a hairnet, called back in accented English, "We on break."

"No break," corrected Warshauer sternly, pointing to the clock on the wall. "Not for three more minutes."

The two women silently donned their aprons again and went back to work. They looked heavyset, but so did everyone on this side. The cut floor was kept at forty-two degrees and layer upon layer of clothing was the only defense against the long, chilled hours. Warshauer watched them for a few more seconds, then turned, motioning for Emmet to follow.

The office was warm and a respite from the constant clattering of metal pans on the tables below. "How's Verna holding up?" asked Warshauer. He smoothed his blond hair that was so neatly coiffed and colored it had earned him the nickname the Clairol Nazi.

"She's okay," replied Emmet.

"My heart breaks for her. But I guess you could see it coming."

"I don't want to talk about it, Bob."

"Oh, come on, Emmet. Frank was a great guy, but he was popping pain killers like they were candy. I think it messed up his head."

Emmet looked away in an effort to cut Warshauer off. "What did you want?" he asked.

"Did you know that he was talking on the sly to an animal rights group?"

"What?"

"Yeah, your buddy Frank was trying to sabotage the plant by bad mouthing us to some animal liberation people."

"What makes you say that?" Emmet's mouth had gone dry.

"Someone saw him taking pictures. And it's come to my attention that a woman from that same animal organization is here in Bragg Falls. These activists are always trying to dig up dirt about farmers and all what else. I guess so they can get more regulations and make it impossible to do our job. She may try to talk to employees at the plant. You know what I'm sayin'?" Assuming Emmet's agreement, he added, "Spread the word. No one is to talk to this gal, right?"

"Outside these walls I can't stop anyone from talking."

"No, but you can let 'em know that if they *do* talk to her they'll be looking for work. And this is not just me, okay? It's coming from corporate direct."

"All right," conceded Emmet. "I'll get the word around."

He was halfway out the door when Warshauer stopped him. "By the way, you being good friends with him and all, did Frank ever tell you about what he was doing?"

"No," Emmet bristled. "No he didn't say anything to me."

"Of course not," reassured the manager. "'Cause if he had, you would have told me."

"Yeah, I would have told you."

Warshauer called out after him, "Oh, the animal person? Her name is Jude Brannock."

Emmet barely registered the name. His brain was burning about what Frank had done. Sure, he didn't like the way things were run, but taking pictures? Talking to an animal rights group? What the fuck ... was he trying to shut down the plant and lose everyone their jobs? Not me, thought Emmet. Godammit, I worked hard for this and I'm gonna keep on moving up the ladder 'til I get out of this stinking place. Shaking off the guilt and the doubt, Emmet went back down and suited up for the kill floor again. He had five minutes to make sure the prods and metal pipes were put away, Vernon was behaving himself, and the line was running smooth. Five minutes until Cimino came down to give a quick look around and conclude, "I don't see any problem here, Chapel." *Yeah, because you wait until somebody like me cleans it all up before you step foot on the hot side, you lazy sonofabitch*! And then Emmet would steel himself to tell Vernon that if he tried to mess with the voltage again he'd write him a citation. He'd suffer the hostile glares of Vernon, Bisbee, Lovato, and all the other workers. At the bar, he'd drink alone or at Warshauer's table. Anything to get off the kill floor where blood and violence earned you maybe twelve bucks an hour and where the chain grated and screeched like a living monster.

CHAPTER 11

I'm just curious," said Jude. "How much would he have to take to kill himself?"

"Depends ... how big was he?" asked CJ.

"Not sure," she answered, checking her rear view mirror to make sure no one had followed her. After driving around trying to get a clear look at the D&M plant, she'd finally pulled over. A manned gate at the entrance prevented her from getting into the parking lot, and the buildings were set too far back from any of the encircling roads to see anything. Now parked on a hill behind the facility, she'd gotten CJ on the phone. "At the house I saw a photo of Frank and I'd say about five-nine, hundred and seventy pounds."

"And if he was on medication for awhile, he'd be opiate tolerant. Hold on."

Jude could hear the clacking of computer keys. "Probably around 500 milligrams," CJ came back.

"They found an empty bottle of 30-milligram pills in his car."

"Well, there you go. Pop fifteen or twenty of those babies or crush them up in a liter of whatever, even if he changed his mind he wouldn't have made it ten minutes."

"Do me a favor, CJ. See what you can find out about a company called PharmaRX." She spelled it for him. "He may have ordered the pain killers from there."

"Okay. What's the plan?"

"I'm sticking around for awhile, see what I can dig up."

"Watch yourself."

"Always do," said Jude. She slipped her cell phone into her pocket, gathered up her backpack, and let Finn out. The plant was somewhere beyond the thick line of trees on the hillside, so she walked along the side of the road until she found an opening onto what looked like an extension of an old logging track. Ignoring the prominently posted no trespassing signs, Jude stuck to the narrow course of pebbly, root-strewn dirt while Finn explored the underbrush on either side.

They had gone about five hundred feet when Finn halted, sniffed the air, and turned his head sharply to look behind them. She followed his gaze but saw nothing. A moment later he did the same thing, alerting her to something or someone.

"What is it, boy?" she asked. And then she heard the sound of dry pine needles crackling under heavy footsteps. Remembering the photos of Roy Mears proudly exhibiting the animals he'd killed, she called Finn close in case there were hunters in the area.

A flash of something shiny through the trees preceded the sight of three figures hurrying down the path. Caroline was in the lead next to a lanky teenage boy with shoulder-length hair; Sophie trailed after them, struggling to keep up.

Caroline brightened when Finn ran to greet her. "Bravo ragazzo," she cooed, ruffling his fur.

Jude didn't know what to make of their appearance. "Ciao, ladies," she said as they approached. "What's up? You following me?"

"Kind of," answered Caroline sheepishly. "We saw you over at the Motor Inn and wondered if you wanted us to show you around. This is Sophie."

"I'm sorry about your dad." Jude shook her plump hand. The girl had her mother's build and big brown eyes, but there was more breadth to her nose and brow where Frank's genes peeked through. She didn't seem to have his moxie, however. Caroline had the edge on that.

"And this is Jack."

The boy barely nodded, taking Jude in with an aloof, half-lidded expression. He was dressed in black jeans and a faded black t-shirt with torn sleeves that revealed tattoos of Celtic symbols on both arms. A silver stud earring in one ear matched the one that Caroline wore through her nose.

"Shouldn't you all be in school?" asked Jude, not really expecting an answer.

"What are you doing here?" Caroline asked by way of a reply.

"Trying to get a look at D&M."

"How come?" asked Sophie.

Jude eyed the trio critically for a moment before saying, "I'm an investigator with an animal protection organization. We think they may be abusing the animals at D&M."

"Well, duh, they're getting killed in there," Jack pointed out.

"Yes, but don't you think it should be done as humanely as possible?" asked Jude.

The girls made quick, furtive eye contact with one another.

Jack struck a nonchalant pose and asked, "So what, you're kind of a private investigator?"

"You could say that."

"Where are you from?"

"Washington, D.C."

"How do we know you are who you say you are?" grilled Jack.

Jude dug in her backpack and handed a card to each of them. "Here you go," she said wryly. "You can send donations to this address, and don't forget to check out the website for tips on becoming a vegetarian."

Scrutinizing the card, Jack raised an eyebrow. "I gather The Kinship refers not just to like minded co-workers, but to the more intangible relationship between man and animal." The kid was smarter than he looked.

"You could say that," Jude tossed over her shoulder, continuing her trek down the path with the teens in tow.

Moments later, the processing facility emerged through the trees on a flat stretch of land below. A high chain link fence topped with curls of barbed wire encircled the complex. But aside from the smell of manure, there were few clues as to what went on inside. They could have been manufacturing toys or pencils in the huge box of a building made of white corrugated aluminum. The only hints were the turbine fans spaced at even intervals on the flat gray roof and the waiting line of livestock transport trucks. Even then, you'd have to know what a livestock truck looked like since it was designed to conceal its cargo. But Jude knew. She had known since that lonely, misty night when she went to investigate the strange sounds inside the eighteen-wheeler.

One of the trucks was starting to back up to the lairage pens, which were covered with a metal roof. But audible inside were the sounds of men shouting "Hey ya, hey ya," as they drove the pigs, one lot at a time, into the pens. Finn stood at heightened attention, ears pricked forward, his tail curved between his legs. He could smell death from where he was.

"I told you about the manure stink. This is where it comes from," pointed out Caroline.

"Not as bad as the lagoons," offered Sophie. "My dad worked at a hog farm before we came here. All the waste goes into these huge, totally gross pits. One time a man fell in and they pulled him right out, but he was already dead."

Jack commented, "You'd have a better chance of surviving a radiation bath."

Meanwhile Jude was pulling out a 35mm camera from her backpack. She adjusted the light settings and began to snap pictures of the plant.

"I don't think you're allowed to do that," warned Caroline.

"Part of my job," said Jude, stepping down to get a better angle.

"But ... but you can't see what goes on from up here."

Glimpsing movement at the loading ramp, Jude affixed a telephoto lens to her camera. Men were running around and shouting, but the truck blocked her view. She squinted through the viewfinder, aware of the girls' secretive whispers behind her and then Jack's voice, "Come on, let's get out of here."

Jude lowered her camera. "Good idea, I'm going to walk around a little."

Sophie quickly followed Jack's lead, but Caroline hesitated as if she wanted to say something, then changed her mind and trotted after her companions. They disappeared back up the path as Jude side-stepped her way down the ridge to take pictures in earnest. She heard the metal ramp on the transport truck clang shut and watched the truck pull away leaving two hogs on the ground outside the pens, pushed off to the side where they wouldn't get in the way.

They were called downers. Unable to move into the chute under their own steam, downers were fairly common. Jude looked through the telephoto lens at the license plate of the truck. If the hogs came from up north this time of year and packed as tightly as they were, some of them might arrive frozen to the sides of the truck, and workers would have to go in to cut them out. Sometimes the weaker ones were attacked or injured, or just too sick to move. No matter the cause, downers were not supposed to go to slaughter until a USDA vet certified that they were disease-free. Jude waited to see what would happen.

A small tractor with a forklift came sputtering around the corner. No veterinarian jumped out, instead a heavy-booted worker carrying a chain. While the motor ran, he wrapped one end of the chain around the pig's rear legs and attached the other end to the forklift. Then he hopped back into the tractor and began dragging the pig along the ground toward an open doorway. Jude could hear the pig's screams from where she stood. She tamped down the anger that rose in her chest and concentrated on doing her job – she checked to make sure the date and time stamp on the camera were correct and started shooting.

The shutter clicks must have covered the rustle of leather behind her, but not Finn's low growl. At his warning, Jude spun around to find herself looking at the barrel end of a gun. Sheriff Ward was pointing his service pistol a few feet to her left where Finn crouched poised and ready to attack. "No, Finn, stay!" she commanded. He stopped growling but continued to fixate on Ward.

"If he comes at me, I'm pullin' the trigger," warned the Sheriff.

Jude's heart raced. "He won't," she told Ward with as much confidence as she could muster.

"How do I know that?" Ward asked warily, still staring at the dog.

"Because I'm telling him not to."

"He always do what you tell him to do?"

"Pretty much."

The Sheriff chuckled uneasily. "*Pretty much* don't make me feel like holstering my weapon."

To demonstrate more control, Jude signaled Finn to lie down. The big dog complied but never took his attention off Ward, who slowly lowered the gun to his side.

Ward licked his lips which had gone dry. "Miss Brannock, I believe? You're on private property, ma'am."

"Oh?"

"You didn't see the no trespassing signs back there?"

"Must have missed them."

"Must have. What are you taking pictures of?"

"Just now, a clear violation of the Humane Slaughter Act," Jude answered, gesturing over her shoulder. "Dragging a non-ambulatory animal to slaughter is prohibited by federal law."

"Well, federal ain't my jurisdiction. So you're going to have leave now." Ward kept his tone cordial as much for Finn's benefit as for hers.

"You also have a state statute prohibiting cruelty to animals and that *would* be your jurisdiction." She also kept her tone cordial, but only because antagonizing law enforcement rarely worked to her or The Kinship's benefit.

"I'm not going to repeat myself," responded Ward stiffly. "And I'm warning you not to come back here or you'll be subject to arrest."

Jude stowed the camera in her backpack and signaled Finn to follow her. She wondered how Sheriff Ward knew she was here. Her suspicion that someone had called him was confirmed when she took a final look over her shoulder and spotted a man with binoculars down by the loading pens – looking straight at her.

* * *

Seldon Marshfield was an uncommon man. He had success and money to spare, but in public was careful not to flaunt either – unusual for a man both short and nondescript. He cultivated a low profile as a happily married man, doting father, and devout churchgoer. As President and CEO of Marshfield Industries, however, he used his power like a scalpel, mercilessly cutting away anything that threatened his business interests.

Today he sat at the head of a conference table with his board of directors. Among them a former U.S. Senator, a senior executive at Dow Chemical, the president of a multi-billion dollar energy company, and a retired federal judge. He had led them through an encouraging internal report showing Marshfield's market share was up in both the commodity and processed food sectors. The recent growth, according to the report, was due to the new "Team Training" they had instituted on all their hog farms and in most of the packing plants, training that used bi-lingual supervisors and certification programs for all the workers. The report buried the real reason for the gains. That information was classified.

Marshfield glanced at his watch. The luncheon was already set up in the dining room; time to move to the last subject. "If you would all turn to tab number seven, Ned Bannerman will give us an overview of our new media campaign. Ned?"

Pages turned while his senior VP picked up the remote for the PowerPoint presentation and began, "I appreciate the opportunity to share with you some of the things we're doing here at Marshfield. Now, of course, you heard earlier that total domestic meat consumption, including pork, beef and chicken is down twelve percent over the last five years. But while the overall pot is shrinking, our market share continues to grow. And we're going to maintain that trend with an aggressive, proactive approach to fight the misperceptions driven by certain animal organizations and fostered in the liberal media. Our new advertising campaign is budgeted at fifteen million dollars. This is a significant investment, about two percent of net profits from last year, and we believe this campaign will help reverse the decline of pork consumption in the U.S. and will drive more consumers to the Marshfield brand by presenting a more accurate vision of our farms and farmers."

He punched a button on the remote that started a video on the wide screen behind him. Cue lilting, tranquil music. A panorama of green fields appeared with clean, pink pigs happily nosing lush grass and clumps of daffodils. The overdub offered up by a sonorous, reassuring male voice averred the commitment by Marshfield and its family of employees to the *quality and well-being of our animals. Here at Marshfield, we believe it is our ethical and moral obligation to keep our animals safe, comfortable and healthy.* The screen changed to show unusually clean pigs in a covered pen, one of them feeding at a trough filled with grain. The wooden floor was spotless. A man and a woman, both wearing light blue aprons walked into the pen. The woman held a stethoscope and put it to the chest of one of the pigs. Obviously satisfied, she smiled. Her partner returned the smile and patted the pig on the head. *We know how to raise healthy pigs at Marshfield, and with our team training we work together to ensure that the quality and well-being of our animals are our highest priorities.* The screen cut to a Norman Rockwell-type family gathering around a holiday table. At the center was a glistening ham. *This is our commitment to you.* The final scene of a pig in the field looking up into the sunlight. *This is our commitment to them.* The music swelled and then faded. There was a smattering of applause by the board members and Seldon beamed.

"We've reconfigured our website as well," added Bannerman, "with an entire section devoted to animal welfare."

The lone woman on the board, a former executive of a major health insurance company, lifted her hand. "I applaud these efforts, Seldon, but a quick question – there was a video released about a month ago, apparently an undercover investigation that showed baby pigs being slammed to the ground amid truly deplorable, filthy conditions. The place was called Heritage Farms. That's not one of ours, is it?"

"Heritage is under contract," Marshfield replied evenly, "but that video was a total fabrication. And in the end, the network that aired the video had to apologize because the animal activist group couldn't prove that it was taken at Heritage."

"*Was* it taken there?" she pressed, eyebrows arched.

"Goodness no," he scoffed. "In fact, the video you just saw – *that* was Heritage Farms." When she responded with a sigh of relief, he smiled broadly, "Why don't we all go to lunch now, and if anyone has further questions, I plan to be available this afternoon."

As the group got up and began talking among themselves, Marshfield took Ned Bannerman by the elbow and instructed him to accompany the board members. Then quietly, he stepped through a side door into a small office where Richard Hillman sat behind a desk watching a live feed of the board meeting on an open laptop.

"I thought the Heritage Farms issue was behind us, Dick," accused Marshfield. "Why is that video surfacing again?"

"One of the animal liberation groups still has it up on their site," responded Hillman.

"Then get the legal department to threaten them. It's got to come down immediately." He shook his head in frustration. "What is Maureen McConnell doing surfing animal liberation sites? Doesn't she have anything better to do? That's probably why Cigna let her go. Did you talk to Bob Warshauer?"

"Yes, and he's getting the word out that no one is to have any contact with Brannock."

Marshfield shifted his small feet and sniffed, as if able to detect any other potential problems from the air. "I want her out of there," he said with finality.

"I understand."

"You told me there are no loose ends with Frank Marino."

"No loose ends," Hillman assured him. "It's been ruled a suicide by the cops and the coroner's office. Case closed."

"And what if he made a copy of the tape that we don't know about?"

"We don't think he did. But if one turns up, we'll know about it and take care of the situation."

"I've got to tell you, Dick, if that thing gets to the media, it's a PR disaster and heads are gonna roll."

"Don't worry. I got it covered."

"I fully expect you do because we just informed the board of an ad campaign that's going to bring *attention* to the animal welfare issue. And I don't intend to get beat by some two-bit animal organization with assets smaller than our bill for paperclips." Marshfield had his hand on the doorknob when he turned back to his Director of Systems Management. A thought made him angry all over again. "These animal people like to make me out as some kind of villain. But you know me, Dick, it's not that I don't care about animals. I do. They've got no right to come after us like we're some kind of outlier when everyone in the industry is doing the same thing. This is a *business* whose function is to respond to demand. Our responsibility is to our stock holders and to the U.S. consumer. Ninety-nine-cent hamburger? Bacon for four dollars a pound? If that's what the American consumer wants, by God, we'll give it to them."

CHAPTER 12

This time when Jude came calling, Verna Marino opened the door herself, although her welcome was far more guarded. The house, too, was different – it seemed to have been turned upside down with shoes, boots, and coats from the front hall closet strewn on the floor, and in the kitchen, drawers open and emptied of their contents.

"Sorry for the chaos," said Verna, trying to put some cheer in her voice. "I need to stay busy, and the house could use a good going over."

Jude noticed the disorder less than she did the obvious changes in Frank's widow. There were dark circles under her eyes and tension around her mouth that had not been there even in the immediate aftermath of his death.

"Are you alright?" asked Jude.

"Holding on. What can I do for you?"

"I wondered if we could talk about Frank."

After a moment's deliberation, Verna opened her hands in a gesture to show she had nothing to hide.

"I only spoke to him a couple of times," started Jude. "I was impressed. He was ... very brave to take a camera inside the plant."

"Like I told you, I wasn't aware of that," Verna stated.

"I'd really like to talk to a few people at the plant about conditions there, but so far, I haven't had much luck. In fact, I'm getting resistance almost everywhere I go. You told me that you worked on the cut floor, so you must have seen quite a bit, and you mentioned some things happening to the animals that were pretty bad."

Verna replied vaguely, "Did I?"

Jude was taken aback. When they first met, Verna was, if not enthusiastic, at least willing to talk about D&M. Now, her equivocation seemed intended to end all conversation. "That's ...that's the impression I got," said Jude flustered. "And your husband obviously felt it was important to show people what's going on at the plant. He contacted us because he was fed up with trying to change the situation from within and knew we could get his footage to the media. At the least of it, he risked his job – maybe more."

"What exactly do you mean by that?" Verna flashed.

"Well, to be honest, I'm having a tough time reconciling his death right on the heels of contacting our organization and offering us his video."

Verna regarded her warily before turning her back and going into the kitchen. She picked up a sheaf of papers from the mess on the kitchen table and thrust it at Jude. "I don't know what you believe," she said. "For myself, *I'd* rather believe my husband overdosed accidentally. It would hurt less than thinking he made a conscious choice to leave us. But all the evidence says that he committed suicide."

Jude scanned the contents, for the most part, copies of police reports. The deputy who found Frank wrote that the car had been parked in a remote area and was locked. An exhaustive search of the interior uncovered a nearly empty bottle of Jim Beam, which acquaintances who knew Frank confirmed was his chosen brand of liquor. The bottle contained traces of crushed oxycodone pills. On it were Frank's and only Frank's fingerprints; same with the empty container of pain killers. No other automobile tracks or footprints were found outside the car, although it had been raining that night and the possibility that they had been washed away could not be ruled out. Customers at the Lazy Cat bar told police that Frank had been there earlier in the evening, but no one could recall the exact time he had left. The most damning, however, was Sheriff Ward's report about what was revealed on Frank's computer: the order to PharmaRX as well as research the victim had apparently done to determine the number of pills he'd have to take to kill himself. Finally, Jude came to a letter from Frank's life insurance company stating that he had taken out the policy less than two years before the date of his death. It wasn't a lot of money for life insurance – ten thousand dollars. But the policy included a two-year suicide clause, and based upon the police and coroner's reports, the company had determined it was not required to pay out.

"So you see," Verna was saying, "I have to accept this."

"You could appeal," said Jude without much conviction.

Verna only wrapped her arms around herself, acknowledging the pain and fruitlessness of such an effort.

"I'm so terribly sorry," said Jude. "If there's anything I can do, please let me know."

Verna answered, "I think the best thing you can do is leave us alone. I'm sorry that you haven't gotten what you wanted. But as I told you, I don't know anything about any video. Perhaps you should just accept things, as I must."

* * *

The lowering sky looked ominous and seemed to reflect Jude's un-easiness about her visit with Verna. She didn't seem like a woman who would so easily resign herself to the insurance company's quick denial or *accept things*, as she'd put it. Did she not share her husband's fighting spirit? But as Jude thought about it and tried to put herself in the widow's position, she imagined that a kind of surrender might be Verna's only way of dealing with the grief. Maybe she felt she was surrendering to God's will. For herself, Jude had no intention of accepting or surrendering to the brutality she'd heard about and now witnessed at D&M. Nor was there anything to prevent her from questioning Frank's suicide. It seemed all too convenient for Marshfield. So after seeing the police reports in Verna's possession, she set off to re-create Frank's last hours. Her first stop was the place where his body had been found.

The reports described a dirt track just off Pigeon Road. Jude found it on her phone's navigation app and after a detour to the motel to get Finn, she drove to the location. About a hundred yards in was the town's old country store, long since abandoned. Jude parked and threw on a jacket. There wasn't much to glean from the location itself, really just a shack with boarded-up windows. From the remains of an above-ground oil tank not far away and a concrete strip out front, it looked as though they had pumped gas here at one time. Now the parking area was overgrown with weeds, a ribbon of yellow police tape twisted on the ground the only evidence that someone had died there.

Why had he chosen this spot? Jude shoved her hands into the pockets of her jacket and studied the derelict building, its rickety covered porch, splintered door, and the rusty soda pop machine too corroded to steal. *Was it because everything here was already lifeless, not worth saving?* She didn't think so. After years of trying to stand up to management, Frank had taken matters into his own hands. It made no sense that he would commit suicide before seeing his efforts play out. A loose piece of plywood nailed to the doorframe of the old store rattled in the wind and made her jump.

The smell of wood smoke drew her attention to the roof of a house tucked away at the end of Pigeon Road. She left the car where it was, whistled to Finn, and walked quickly toward the house. It was fronted by a carefully tended hedge and a bright red mailbox. Beyond them, the property opened to a clearing that burst with color and life. In the center sat a fenced vegetable garden, boasting the last of the season's sunflowers and waves of kale and red chard. Nestled alongside, a hut stored rows of gardening tools and pickling jars, and nearby was a cozy red barn with its doors open. A couple of hens scratched in the dirt by the opening, but when they caught sight of Finn, scrambled inside. Drawn to the scent of sweet hay, Jude followed them.

"Hello?" she called out. No one answered.

The only sounds were the muted clop of hooves on the wooden floor and chomping teeth. Two fat sheep in a converted horse stall glanced up briefly before returning to their methodical chewing. From the back came soft grunts, and Jude followed them to a boarded pen, where a large pot-bellied pig lay on her side suckling six baby pigs, each of whom was small enough to fit in a shoebox.

As Jude crouched down to get a better look, two of the spotted piglets tripped over each other to get to her. Curious and friendly, they pushed their tender, pink snouts through the rail openings. Entranced, Jude held her hand close but didn't try to touch them, not wanting to make their mother anxious. But the sow only lifted her head briefly.

Finn padded over and sniffed the piglets, who seemed delighted to meet this strange new creature. Their yips drew their siblings over and soon they were all trying to jump on Finn. He gave Jude a baleful look that asked, "What do I do now?" and she laughed. With their short, uncoordinated legs, the babies bounced around the wood chip bedding, falling over one another, and occasionally hopping over to smoosh their noses into Jude's hand. Mama sow looked on patiently, perhaps glad to have a break from the kids; one could almost see a smile on her face. Someone had put a soccer ball in the pen, which the piglets rolled and tackled, and before long, Jude found herself cross-legged on the ground, lost in their joy of play.

As her shoulders and the muscles in her forehead relaxed, she tried to experience the world through the youngsters' eyes ... the fascination with a clump of straw or pleasure in finding a bit of food. As often happened, Jude was struck with the mystery of animals. They inhabited a world no human would fully understand – a bond with the earth, the rain, the smells carried on the breeze, and critically, no matter prey, friend or foe, an intrinsic recognition of the value of other animals. That was something humans did not possess. Ever since she'd been a child, Jude yearned to live in that animal universe, even for a moment, released from the constraints of her past and the doubts she carried about whether she could really make a difference.

"Aren't they cute?" asked a voice behind her.

Jude quickly turned her head to see a sturdy woman with white wisps of hair sticking out from under a gardening hat. Dressed comfortably in baggy pants tucked into knee-high muck boots, she looked familiar.

Blushing at her obvious intrusion, Jude jumped to her feet, causing the piglets to scamper away. "I'm sorry to barge in like this," she said. "I didn't see anybody, and I called out, but–"

"Not to worry, dear," said the woman kindly. "I know you. We met at Verna Marino's house. I'm Oma Burney."

Now Jude remembered where she had seen her. "Of course, after Frank's funeral."

Reminded of it, distress clouded Oma's lined face. "Have you seen Verna recently?" she asked.

"Just this morning."

"I was supposed to see her at Bible study, but I couldn't make it. I pray for her. Frank was devoted to her and Sophie."

The sense of unease that Jude felt when she left Verna intensified; she tried to grab onto what it was that nagged at her, but was quickly distracted by the gang of baby pigs who were once again vying for attention at her feet.

"How old are they?"

"Almost four weeks now. Would you like to hold one? I've gotten them used to being handled."

"May I?"

Oma reached down and picked up one of the spotted piglets and turned him over to a delighted Jude, saying, "That's Truman. I name them after authors I've just finished. That there is Toni, Dashiell, Jonathan ... though I didn't like Franzen's last book too much."

"Hello, Truman," laughed Jude. She cuddled the eight-pound youngster against her shoulder. His skin was like a soft-bristled brush and tickled her as he wiggled in her arms and rubbed his snout against her neck. It seemed unfathomable that in hog farms across the country, babies just like these were wrenched from their mothers, tails, teeth and testicles clipped, then crowded into indoor pens or crates where they would never set foot on grass or feel the sun. Jude put him back extra gently into the pen as the mama lumbered to her feet and came over to snort a greeting.

"Watch this," said the older woman. She reached into her pocket and pulled out a small bag of apple pieces. "Sit, Emily," she commanded. The pig lowered her rear end to the ground and received her treat. "Down." Emily lay down on her side. By this time, Finn had come circling around, waiting for *his* treat and Oma obliged with a slice of apple that he took from her hand.

Oma scratched her pig under the chin. "Okay, go outside." She pointed and Emily did as she was told, her piglets scampering after her.

"Oh my word," exclaimed Jude. "I knew pigs were smart, but that's amazing."

"She knows more than that," replied Oma. "But you certainly didn't come to see my pigs."

"If I'd known about them, I would have," Jude assured her. "But I actually came to see where Frank died, and then I saw your house. I wondered if anyone had seen him that night."

"I'm afraid I didn't. I'm usually in bed by nine-thirty." She gazed at a place beyond Jude's head for a moment, then added, "It's very disturbing that he chose that spot right down the street. I couldn't tell you why."

"He might not have chosen it," suggested Jude.

"What do you mean?"

Seeing the alarm on Oma's face, Jude hurriedly reconsidered her answer and said, "Oh, I don't know, perhaps the choice wasn't made consciously." But what she really wanted to say was that perhaps someone had chosen it for him.

Chapter 13

It was hard to drag herself away from the warmth in Oma's barn, but Jude wanted to get the photos of the downer hog to Gordon before he left for the day. Out on Pigeon Road, the wind had picked up, bringing with it the first drops of a cold rain. As she got closer to her car, she noticed something odd. A few steps later, she saw the letters on the side – something spray painted. Jude began to run.

The writing was sprayed in a messy scrawl that was still tacky to the touch. YOUR TURN SOW! But the other message was even more sickening. Fresh blood had been thrown over the front of the car. It was still dripping into the well of the windshield and down the fenders, pooling on the ground. Jude gagged from the smell. In a daze, she circled the car. Whoever had done this was gone, but she hadn't been at Oma Burney's place for that long, nor had she told anyone where she was going. Evidently, someone was tracking her movements. Anger began to take the place of shock. It took a moment before she realized it had started to rain in earnest, so she dashed to the abandoned shack to take cover and call the police. While she waited for them to show up, she contacted the office.

"What are you going to do?" asked CJ. "You want me to page Gordon?"

Jude sighed, "No, just let him know when you see him. I'm waiting for the cops now."

"You think you should come back home? It could get dangerous for you."

"It won't be the first time I've been threatened and it sure won't be the last, but the spray paint royally pisses me off. I don't know how to get it off and meanwhile, that writing is going to draw attention to me everywhere I go."

"What about the blood. Is it human, you think?"

"Probably not, but I'm sure the cops will get it tested."

"That's gross. What do you make of the writing?"

"You mean, my *turn*, as in turn to get stunned and shackled?"

"Yah, and maybe get your throat slit."

"I don't know, CJ. Most of the time this kind of thing is all bluff and bluster. If somebody wants to get to me, they can – I'm not hiding. This is meant to scare me away."

"Maybe it should."

Jude saw the nose of a deputy squad car rounding the corner. "I have to go," she said.

"One quick thing," interjected CJ. "A little while ago, you got a call from a girl named ... Caroline? She wants you to come to dinner at her house tonight. Why'd she call here?"

"I gave her my business card. Did she leave a number?"

"Yeah."

"Okay, could you text it to me and I'll call her back."

A young, black deputy emerged from his car and warily circled Jude's wagon. "You know who did this?" he asked.

"No, not really."

He got around to the spray painted side and squinted at it. "What does that mean, *Your Turn Son?*"

"I think it says *Sow.*"

"Sow, as in female pig?" He went back to the squad car and retrieved a kit from the trunk. From it he took a small vial and scraped some of the blood into it. "This just happened, right?"

Jude gave him an approximate time line: when she left her car and how long she'd been away. He asked a few more questions and she answered truthfully.

"You're an animal activist?" he confirmed. "Guess someone around here is not too happy about that."

"Guess not."

The rain was getting heavier, sending Jude and the deputy to the store's leaky front porch. He took out a notebook to write up a report, but Jude couldn't offer much more than she already told him. Soon, sheets of water were pelting from the sky. Finn took cover as well, spraying them both as he shook his coat. They watched the blood turn pink and run off the car, mixing with the dirt, then forming rivulets that took the rust-brown water into the weeds. The warning scrawled on the side of the car remained.

Pocketing his notebook, the deputy said, "Good news is ... you're getting a free car wash. Bad news ... probably have to get your car repainted. I just had mine done, and with the primer it cost nearly eight hundred bucks."

* * *

At the motel, Jude called Caroline and accepted the dinner invitation for her and Finn. Her familiarity with threats notwithstanding, the message on Pigeon Road had been received loud and clear. It was creepy and more than a little unsettling, and she figured it would do her good to get out of the motel where her anxiety would only fester.

Jude showered and changed into a pair of black jeans and a gray scoop-neck sweater that yielded a glimpse of the hollows above her collarbone. She had some time before she had to be at Caroline's and decided to pay a visit to the Lazy Cat. It was the last place anyone had seen Frank. And if it was a drinking hole for D&M workers, she might find someone willing to talk.

She walked by a few curious stares before slipping onto one of the Lazy Cat barstools. The five o'clock news played softly on the overhead TV, but the bartender was the only one watching. In his early thirties and boasting a thick mustache, he pushed off the counter and came over to see what she wanted.

"You have anything on tap besides Bud or Coors?" she asked.

"Not on tap, but I've got a bottled pale ale from a local brewery that might just suit you."

"I'll try it," said Jude.

He brought back the beer and poured it into a tall glass, letting just a bit of foam drip down the side. She took a sip. "Nice. Not too light with a little citrus pop."

That earned her a smile. He appreciated anyone who recognized a good beer, and an attractive girl made it even better. "I like 'em heavier on the malt myself, but that's a good one. Most of the folks around here wouldn't know a microbrew from piss in a can." He held out his hand. "My name's Nick, I'm part-owner here."

"Hi, I'm Jude. Wondered if you might be able to help me."

"If I can."

"Were you here last Friday night?"

"I'm here just about every night."

"Did you know a man named Frank Marino?"

Nick drew back slightly and fingered his mustache. "Sure, I knew him."

"Then I guess you know that he committed suicide last Friday."

"You a reporter?" he asked, edging away. He didn't want any bad publicity.

"No, nothing like that," said Jude quickly. "We were ... working on something together and I was supposed to meet him the other day, and then I found out..."

"Yeah, well, he was a regular."

"And Frank was here last Friday?"

"The whole crew was here."

"The crew?" asked Jude.

"We serve a lot of the guys from the D&M plant. That's where Frank worked."

"Do you remember his demeanor? Did he seem upset or bothered by anything?"

"Like I told the cops, I try to keep my eyes open and most of the time I can spot a fight brewing, but to tell you if some guy is depressed or something, I wouldn't know. And we were real busy that night. I had my hands full."

"Anything out of the ordinary that you recall? I mean, Frank being a regular and all, he probably stuck to a routine."

Nick frowned, trying to think. "Well, I saw him at the bar, he got a drink." He cocked his head. "Come to think of it, he doesn't normally sit at the bar. He's usually with Emmet and a few of the other guys."

"Emmet?"

"Yeah, Emmet Chapel. They were pretty tight and the two of them usually sit at a table over there." Nick pointed across the room.

"Does Emmet work at D&M?"

"As long as I can remember."

"Anyone else you know work there? Maybe I could talk to them."

Before Nick could respond, someone called his name. He responded to a tall, heavyset black man waiting to order at the far end of the bar. Nick held up a finger to let him know he'd be right over, then he turned back to Jude.

"If you want to talk to someone who works at the plant, you might try Howard Bisbee," he said, nodding to the big man. "He knew Frank."

Jude picked up her beer and wandered down to where Bisbee leaned against the bar. She put him in his mid to late forties, graying around the temples with deep lines cut into his broad face. After introducing herself, she asked if he knew Frank Marino or Emmet Chapel.

Bisbee squinted down at her. "Mind telling me who you are again?"

"I'm with an organization called The Kinship. Frank contacted me, wanting to talk about D&M."

Bisbee shook his head. "Sorry, I got nothin' to say to you." He picked up his pitcher of beer and walked away.

Jude trailed after him. "Please, I just want to ask you a couple of questions."

"Miss, you look like a nice person," said Bisbee. "But I ain't gonna talk to you."

"Why not?"

"Because I don't talk to animal rights people."

Jesus. What the hell was going on? Was her picture plastered all over town like a wanted poster?

Fighting off a growing desperation, Jude tried another tack. "I'm not here to ask you about D&M, Mr. Bisbee," she said. "I was

told you were a friend of Frank's, and I'm only trying to understand why he committed suicide."

Bisbee seemed torn between walking away and trying to understand the same thing. He glanced quickly around the room,
gauging how safe it was to talk, then heaved the sigh of a man who
wanted to put the entire episode behind him and said, "The man's
back was bad, and I know for sure he was addicted to pain killers.
He couldn't bend over or lift anything without 'em. And anyone
around here can tell you those things ain't a long term solution.
Frank'd worked for Marshfield practically his whole life, different
locations, but always with hogs. He didn't have no college education, didn't have any other trade that I know of."

"So you're saying he might have taken his own life because he
was concerned about how he'd make a living?"

"I'm sayin' he dint have many options." His eyes flickered to
the doorway and suddenly, like a door slamming, he shut down.

Two men had come in and were making their way over. One of
them wore thick, black glasses; the other was an older gentleman
with a kindly, ruddy face.

"How's it going, Howard?" asked the older man.

"Not bad."

"And who might this lovely young lady be?"

"I'm Jude Brannock."

"Glad to meet you, dear. My name is Lawrence Cimino. This is
Patrick LaBrie," he said, indicating his companion.

Jude recognized Cimino's name from her files on D&M. He
was the on-site veterinarian and the senior representative from the
USDA. She couldn't even muster a thin smile, not after what she'd
seen from the ridge. "Mr. Cimino, I was actually going to look you
up," she said.

He raised a bushy eyebrow.

"You see, I was outside the plant today and witnessed a downer hog being dragged with a chain. I wondered if anyone had reported that to you."

"Ah, you're with the animal welfare group. No, I received no such report," said Cimino innocently. She felt sure that he knew exactly who she was before she introduced herself.

Jude continued, "It's considered an egregious violation of the Humane Slaughter Act."

"I'm well aware of the act's provisions and I'm sure you couldn't have seen what you claim, Miss Brannock. We take good care of our animals."

"Not only did I see it, I photographed it."

"And just where did you take this photograph?"

"From the ridge overlooking the lairage pens."

Cimino clucked like a disapproving grandmother. "That's private property, my dear, belonging to the Marshfield corporation. You could get into trouble for trespassing on private property. But since you tell me you witnessed this alleged violation, I'll surely look into it."

Something about the outwardly sweet old man who treated this information so casually was repellent to Jude. And he was a vet, trained to take care of animals, no less. She turned her attention to Patrick LaBrie. "Are you also with the USDA?"

When he acknowledged that he was, she asked boldly, "Mr. LaBrie, are you aware of non-ambulatory hogs going into the slaughter line?"

He blinked behind his thick-framed glasses. "Downers? Absolutely not."

"Do you get over to the lairage pens, sir?" demanded Jude.

Cimino chuckled as if she had made a joke, then turned away and steered LaBrie toward the bar. Jude was left standing with Bisbee.

"Might as well go home," he said softly. "Ain't no one going to talk to you about the hogs or anything else. And you keep at it, you stand to make some enemies."

She pressed her hands against her tired eyes and said, "Think I already have."

* * *

On her way to Caroline's house, Jude stopped at a local market, searching for something to bring with her. She was just coming out, a bunch of pre-packaged daisies in hand, when she spotted the young man who had approached her outside the diner. He was driving a van into the parking area of the hardware and feed supply across the street. She was about to start after him when he and two men got out and went into the store.

Hoping that "Juan" might come out solo, she crossed the street to linger casually in the parking area. There she noticed a parking sticker on the van's front window. It looked current and had been issued by a place called King's Court, more specifically for space twenty-seven. Jude filed the information away and left before Juan and his friends returned.

CHAPTER 14

A small boy playing with stones squatted in the driveway. He'd arranged them in a line, lofting the frontrunners at a plastic kiddie pool half filled with stale, brown water. One by one they went in with a satisfying plop. So engrossed in his game, he didn't see Jude drive up to the curb. But at the sound of the car door closing, he lifted his head to look at her with the same sapphire blue eyes as his sister.

"Hi. Are you Caroline's brother?" asked Jude.

He nodded and studied her for a moment. Suddenly, he spied Finn and forgetting Jude and his rocks, jumped up and pointed at the car. "Is that a dog or what?" he wanted to know. Finn's large head emerged through the open window of the Subaru.

"Don't worry, I won't let him out of the car."

But rather than appearing relieved, the boy looked crushed. "Can't I play with him?" he appealed.

"Don't see why not." Jude let Finn out and watched both dog and exuberant boy gallop around the yard.

At that moment, Caroline came to the front door and her face brightening with anticipation, exclaimed, "You're here! Come on in. My mother's inside, she just got home from work." She ushered her guest into the kitchen where a woman in a blue Walmart uniform stood in front of the open oven, poking a fork into a sweet potato. Without turning around, she called out irritably, "When did you put these in, Caroline? They're not even close to being done. Oh!" She caught sight of Jude and quickly wiped her damp hands on her uniform.

"You must be Caroline's friend," she said. "I'm Alice Chapel."

Chapel. Caroline had never said her last name, and in an instant, Jude made the connection. Emmet Chapel – close friend of Frank Marino and the man at his graveside – was Caroline's father.

"I ... these are for you," said Jude, reddening slightly and thrusting out the flowers.

"Thank you, they're lovely." Alice took them and rummaged through a cabinet for something to put them in. She found a chipped vase and filled it with water.

"I hope I'm not putting you out," said Jude.

"Not at all." Alice's tone was warm enough, but her pinched, lipstick-faded smile spoke volumes – a tough day in customer service followed by her daughter's announcement as soon as she walked through the door that they were having company. But she'd been brought up right and tried to make Jude feel comfortable. "We're glad you could come," she added.

Caroline dismissed her mother, saying, "You go change, Mom. I'll take care of dinner."

Alice must have heard something in her daughter's tone because all at once she seemed self-conscious in her polyester uniform, aware that in Caroline's eyes it carried the stain of failure.

"Sure, I'll be right back. Honey, get those potatoes back in the oven, please?"

When she was gone, Caroline shifted her feet nervously.

Not completely at ease herself, Jude pointed to the flowers. "Shall I put these on the table?" Then after a moment, she said, "Your mom's nice."

"She's okay. I get along with her most of the time, probably better than a lot of kids I know. She gets on me for certain things, like these," Caroline proudly pushed her hair back to show off the multiple ear piercings. "And she worries too much. But she's got a lot on her mind. I ... uh, wondered if I could ask you something."

"Sure, what is it?"

"It's about what you do and all."

"Being an animal welfare investigator?"

Caroline nodded. "You have to get evidence, right? I mean, people doing stuff to animals and maybe–"

A high-pitched squeal from outside interrupted Caroline, and Jude put up her hand. "Hold that thought. I'd better go check on your brother. Be right back."

The sound that had come from the yard, however, was one of delighted play. Will and Finn were having a grand time. The six-year-old had found a baseball and fashioned a new game that included Finn and the dirty water in the kiddie pool. Jude wasn't sure if Alice would find the game nearly as amusing, and she was relieved when Alice came out on the front landing and took it all in without complaint. Now with her hair pulled back in a ponytail and wearing jeans and a sweater, Caroline's mother looked more comfortable, although her half-smile still seemed forced.

"He's big, but he's good with kids," Jude assured her. "I can put him in the car if you like." Because of his size, vouching for Finn's good intentions was almost a habit for her.

"It's fine," said Alice. "Will adores dogs."

There was an awkward silence, neither of them terribly good with small talk. Finally, away from her daughter's judgmental presence, something in Alice seemed to loosen. "I'm pleased that Caroline has made a friend," she said. "When I got home, she told me she met an 'amazing' woman who came *all the way* from Washington. You're quite the celebrity to her."

"She's an interesting girl."

"It's nice to see her looking forward to something. Caroline's been kind of depressed lately." Alice paused, considering how much to say. "Her schoolwork is suffering."

Jude could offer only a sympathetic glance in return; it didn't feel like her place to tell her that her daughter was out running at the state park instead of attending school.

Alice continued, "She seems so angry all the time, and she has ... dark thoughts." It might have been the loneliness of carrying the load by herself or the possibility that this young woman whom her daughter clearly admired might have some answers, but Alice blurted out, "She's seems obsessed with death and we don't understand why. She's not sick. It just seems unnatural to have such a sense of foreboding all the time."

Jude listened, speech eluding her.

"But she's seeing a doctor. I think she'll be all right, don't you?"

Luckily, Caroline called them in for dinner, saving Jude from having to respond. They arranged themselves around the kitchen table that Caroline had set for the four of them. Her mother had told her not to wait for Emmet – his schedule was "unpredictable" these days and he could get something to eat later. In honor of her guest, Caroline had put out cloth napkins and a candle next to the flowers. It sat in a misshapen clay holder that was one of Will's kindergarten projects and every time the table moved, it wobbled precariously.

The teenager's turn to cook that night had resulted in some version of Hamburger Helper, baked yams and a salad. She watched Jude expectantly while Alice served.

"Sorry, I don't eat meat," said Jude, holding up an apologetic hand. "But the potatoes look great and with a salad, that'll be fine for me."

"You're a vegetarian?" asked Alice, her serving spoon poised over the casserole dish.

"Yes, actually I don't eat any animal food."

"None?" Alice quizzed. "However do you get your protein?"

"Various ways, legumes, soy, stuff like that."

"What's *animal* food?" broke in Will to no one in particular.

"Why?" Alice asked perplexed.

"I work for an animal welfare organization," said Jude. "But even if I didn't, I couldn't support the way farm animals are treated."

"Oh. Caroline did tell me you worked with animals, but I thought it was rescuing cats and dogs."

"We do some of that, yes. But we also try to prevent abuse to farm animals."

Caroline took the serving spoon from her mother's hand and used it to scrape her portion of Hamburger Helper back into the serving dish. "I've decided I'm not going to eat meat."

Her mother smiled indulgently. "You're a teenager and have different dietary needs, honey."

"No, I'm going vegetarian," insisted Caroline.

Will, who had been watching his big sister carefully, kneeled up on his chair and shoveled his casserole back. "I'm going vege ... vege-train, too," he announced.

"Don't be ridiculous, Will," Alice admonished, replenishing his plate. "You need your protein."

He crossed his arms defiantly. "It's animal food," he said with a scowl.

"Oh, for God's sake," snapped Alice.

Wincing at the trouble she was causing, Jude said, "I'm sorry."

"I don't understand, what is the problem? We have to eat meat and chicken."

"Who says, mother?" demanded Caroline. "They're living, breathing creatures. Why should they die so we can eat them?"

"Finn is a dog and I wouldn't eat him," said Will somberly.

"No one's asking you to, Will," insisted his mother impatiently. "Eating chicken and hamburger is completely different."

"I don't believe it is," said Jude softly.

"She's right, Mom," asserted Caroline. "You have no idea how badly the pigs are treated."

"Slaughtering hogs is just something we have to do," insisted her mother.

"It isn't something we *have* to do. And you have no freaking idea what really happens to them," Caroline admonished, her voice rising in anger. "You don't *want* to know, just like everybody else around here. It's all a dark, horrible secret that nobody in this town wants to fuckin' see!"

"What's going on?" boomed Emmet from the doorway. He'd heard his daughter cursing from outside and his face was like thunder.

Alice jumped up from the table, flustered. "Emmet ... this is ... uh, Caroline's friend."

Jude looked up at the broad-shouldered man who filled the kitchen doorway, struck by the intensity of his blue eyes. He scanned the table, taking in the situation, and then his gaze rested on Jude.

"Nice to meet you," he said uncertainly. "Are you from the school?" They'd gotten a few calls about Caroline's truancy and he thought they might have decided to send someone to the house.

"Did you see the dog?" asked Will hopefully.

Emmet's face creased into a smile. "Didn't see any dog, sport," he said. "But I saw a grizzly bear out in the car. He yours?" he asked Jude.

Will guffawed. "It's not a bear, Dad, it's a dog. You can't put a bear in a car."

The adults laughed while Emmet stepped over to the sink and methodically washed up. After wiping them dry with paper towel he held out his hand to Jude. "Hi, I'm Emmet. I guess you know my wayward daughter?"

"I do," said Jude, shaking his strong hand. "I'm Jude Brannock."

Like a light suddenly extinguished, the smile faded from his face. "The animal rights lady? I ... uh ... I'm afraid I'm going to have to ask you to leave."

"What?" Caroline burst out.

"Look, I'm a floor supervisor at D&M and we're under strict orders not to talk to you. What we do and what you do are just not compatible."

"Emmet, she's a guest," Alice pointed out sternly.

Caroline threw her napkin on the table. "Dad, what are you doing? I invited her."

"I'm sorry." Emmet stood firm. "But I could get fired if anyone even saw you here."

Alice admonished him under her breath, "This is not right. She's a guest in our house, and we don't have to talk about your work."

Keeping his eyes trained on Jude, he said harshly, "I know about Frank contacting you, and I know about the videotape – if he really did make one. It's not here. I don't know where it is and neither does Verna, so I'd appreciate it if you'd let us all alone. Nothing good is going to come of it."

Alice's eyes darted from her husband to Jude. "Emmet, what does Frank have to do–"

"I'm sorry," he broke in. "Please leave."

"So am I," said Jude. "I understand." She got up from her chair.

"No!" cried Caroline.

Emmet stepped back to let Jude pass, and she reached over to take Caroline's hand. "Can you walk me to the car?"

The teenager burst into angry sobs, turning on her father. "I can't believe you're doing this. God, I hate you!"

Alice put her head in her hands to drown out her daughter's wails of protest as she accompanied Jude down the driveway. Then the sounds of a car door and wheels on the dirt. Caroline did not reappear.

In the silent kitchen, Emmet sat in his daughter's chair and began to help himself to the casserole and potatoes while Will watched him expectantly, his lower lip trembling. After a moment, Alice picked up her head, her face gray with sorrow. "She was happy, Emmet," she said softly. "She was happy tonight."

CHAPTER 15

At another dinner table eighty miles away, Richard Hill-man gazed appreciatively at his wife. After her golf game, she'd had her hair and nails done. He liked that she kept herself fit and impeccably groomed. Tonight they were hosting three of her friends and their husbands whom Hillman didn't hate. The weather on the patio had been perfect for cocktails, and now the dining room in their Georgian style home glittered from the crystal chandelier down to the polished silver. Hillman was content.

At least he was until his cell phone vibrated in the chest pocket of his sport coat. With as little fanfare as possible, he checked the screen.

"Excuse me," he said to the woman at his right.

His wife spotted the move. "Not tonight, Rich, dear," she moaned with a smile.

"It's nothing, love. I'll be right back." He strode across the front hall into his study and closed the doors behind him. Standing at one of the eight-foot windows overlooking the patio and the rarely used swimming pool, he hit the callback button. The phone rang once.

"This better be important, Bloom," said Hillman. "My wife is having a dinner party."

"Two things you should know." Bloom wasn't one to apologize. "Marino took out a life insurance policy eighteen months ago. It's got a two-year suicide clause."

"Shit. Are they going to open an investigation?"

"I doubt it. The coroner's ruling makes it a done deal. But Brannock is hanging around. Looks like she's tracing Marino's path. She went to the meet spot and then to the Lazy Cat. Talking to the widow, too. She may have suspicions."

Hillman watched a few leaves drift into the pool and get sucked into the filtering system. Finally, he said, "Well, I trust she won't find anything."

"She won't."

"As far as the insurance, I'll contact Warshauer and authorize some kind of payment to Marino's widow. He can call it a pension or death benefit, but he's got to *shut down* the communication between her and Brannock. I'm still concerned about whether Marino made a copy of the video. I know what he told you, but maybe Brannock's sticking around because she knows something we don't. She is not to get her hands on it."

Bloom abruptly ended the call, and Hillman felt the expensive merlot he'd opened for dinner reassert itself up the back of his throat. He'd made a fine living for himself insulating Seldon Marshfield and his firm from trouble. And he would do whatever was necessary to keep it that way. He gave a final look out at the pool receding into the darkness and strode back to his dinner guests. All options were on the table.

* * *

The glint of an old hubcap dangling on the chain link fence drew Jude's attention to the sign which was partially obscured by overgrown weeds. Called Kings Court, the trailer park was anything but – streetlamps were out, garbage cans upended, and more than a few dogs ran loose. She crept along a dirt road that wound between rows of trailers until she saw number twenty-seven. Parked in front was the van she'd seen "Juan" drive to the hardware store. But leery of drawing attention to him, she drove further down to a clearing where worn, plastic toys littered the cracked earth. Across the way, three Hispanic men barely out of their teens sat around a picnic table drinking beer. Jude's arrival elicited some comments and laughter, but the throbbing bass of a Chicano rap group blaring from their radio drowned out their words. She left Finn in the car with the windows cracked and walked back.

Jude knocked on the trailer door. As she hoped, Juan answered, though his eyes widened when he saw who it was. He looked past her anxiously to see if she was alone, then hurried her into the trailer and quickly closed the door. The small space was filled with the smell of cumin and fried onions and Jude's rumbling stomach reminded her she hadn't had any dinner. A baby wailed somewhere in the back.

"I would have called, but I didn't have your number," said Jude apologetically. "I know it's asking a lot, but I happened to see the sticker on your van at the hardware store. I was hoping we could talk."

He shoved his hands in his pockets, looking as though he deeply regretted starting up a conversation in the first place. A pretty woman in her twenties with a baby on her hip swung into view and looked distrustfully back and forth from her husband to Jude as she tried to coax the baby into a better mood.

"This is my wife," said Juan, clearly unhappy to have to make the introduction.

Jude introduced herself and added, "I met your husband outside the diner and he started to tell me about the animals and what's happening at D&M."

She shot her husband a dark glance.

"Ella es una amiga de Frank," he said softly. "Él le pidió que viniera aquí."

"A venir acá?" she asked with evident disapproval. "A nuestra casa?

"No. To Bragg Falls."

They argued in quiet tones for a few moments, their positions plain. Juan was willing to talk – his wife wasn't. Jude spoke a little Spanish and was able to pick out a few words as he reminded his wife how difficult it was for them when they first started working at the plant and how Frank had helped her get the job with steady hours. How Frank never lied to them, unlike so many others. At one point, he blurted out in English that Frank "had my back," as he did with the other "Mexicanos" who everyone else treated "como shit." They owed him a debt and that if Frank cared about the animals that much, they should honor his wishes and talk to this woman.

His wife finally conceded, "Give me a minute." She returned in less than that with the baby sucking furiously on a bottle. She left him in a car seat on a bench at the built-in dining table and resumed her preparations in the kitchenette. "We will eat now. You join us?" she asked. "Only rice and beans."

"I would love to," said Jude, meaning it.

Over the fragrant, spicy food, Jude explained how Frank had

come to call her. She learned that "Juan's" real name was Daniel; he had moved to Texas at age nineteen and was hoping to open a restaurant someday. His wife was named Abelina. She was from Mexico City where she had gotten her degree in nursing. But with no luck finding a decent paying job, she had come north to be with Daniel and D&M had hired her to work in casings.

"What do you do in casings?" asked Jude.

"Clean out hog intestines for sausage."

"Not easy, I suppose."

"You get used to it. At first, it's terrible – the blood, the shit, excuse me, and the worms. They are the worst."

"Roundworms?"

"Yes, many hogs have them, and they're big, sometimes a foot long. When I was new, the others, they can be really mean, shoving the worms in my face. But I stood up to them and they leave me alone now."

"It's a little like life inside a prison," Daniel interjected with a faint smile. "You gotta be tough and wear your game face."

Abelina tossed her ponytail over her shoulder and shrugged. "At least I can work a single shift," she said. "I come home and take care of the baby. Frank work that out for us. Daniel sometime, they make work double shift, one at the tank, then the cleaning crew. Seventeen hours straight, only time to sleep for a few hours, then go back."

Jude turned her attention to Daniel. "At the diner, you started to tell me that things were happening to the workers and the animals. What kind of things?"

He hesitated, his eyes resting on his young, sleeping son, until his wife nudged him, saying, "Go ahead, tell her."

Daniel blew out a sigh and opened up. "Okay. I work sometimes at the scalding tank so I see the hogs before they're cut up. I see what kind of shape they're in. You can tell if they've been dragged because they have scrape marks all over or wounds where they put the hooks to pull them – sometimes in the nose or the mouth."

Although she had not eaten since lunch, Jude's appetite disappeared.

"The most important thing is to keep the line going," Daniel continued. "If there's a crippled hog in the chute or one that refuses to go, it's going to stop production. So we got to beat them and use the electric prods to keep them moving. Then sometimes, they trample each other to get away."

"Have you complained about these things to management or the USDA inspectors?" asked Jude.

Daniel shook his head. "You have to understand," he said. "I'm okay in this country, but Abelina doesn't have her green card. And we came to this town because I have relatives, some of them work at D&M, too. I open my mouth, I get them fired. When you're hungry for the work, you don't push back."

"It's not just the animals," Abelina broke in. "At my station, a woman died of meningitis and two others got it from bacteria the hogs carry. The inspectors are supposed to watch for hurt pigs or the ones that are sick, but they miss many things. Mr. Warshauer, he calls everything an *isolated incident*." Her mouth twisted in an expression that said none of the workers believed that.

Although Daniel had just explained their situation, Jude felt compelled to ask. "If I wrote all this up, would you be willing to sign an affidavit?"

Both of them shook their heads in no uncertain terms and Jude knew it would be pointless to try and convince them otherwise. She reached out and tenderly stroked their son's chubby fist. "How aware is management of immigration status?" she asked.

Daniel chuckled. "Let me put it this way: to come over the border is expensive, but for an extra hundred bucks you can get a fake ID. You want a job at a place like D&M, that's all they ask for – that and a heartbeat."

Jude asked suddenly, "Did you know Frank was taking video inside?" She watched to see their reaction, and they both seemed genuinely surprised.

"I didn't know that," said Daniel, finally. "But it's possible that *someone* suspected because last week they were doing bag searches at the end of each shift."

"Looking for a camera you think?" prompted Jude.

"Well, they do that if they think someone is stealing meat, but yeah, maybe looking for a camera." Daniel paused. "He made the video to give to you?"

Jude nodded, then broached the question she never had the chance to ask Frank, "Why do you think he did it? Bring in a camera, I mean. At the diner you told me he stood up to management, so he was already doing something. But bringing in a camera and taking video would have gotten him fired. He couldn't afford that, could he?"

Abelina answered, "You could see something building inside him. Frank write letters about the abuse. He send them to some big politicians, but I don't think they write back. When something bad happened on our side of the floor, he tell us, 'Just be patient, they're gonna send someone down. Got to hold on.' I think he got tired of holding on."

Daniel had been quietly tracing the edge of his napkin while Abelina spoke. Now he lifted his head and said, "Couple months ago, maybe less, we were standing in line waiting to get our gear and he looked bad. I thought he was mad at me for some reason because he wouldn't say nothing. But then all of a sudden he turns around and comes up real close," imitating Frank's fierce glare, Daniel thrust his face toward Jude, "and says, 'if you love your wife and your baby, get out of here now before it's too late, before you stop caring.'"

"Caring about what?" asked Jude.

"About *life*," replied Daniel, as if she ought to have known.

"You think he stopped caring about his own life?" asked Jude.

Finn began to bark in the distance and she heard a warning in his tone. "I better go," she said. "I appreciate everything you've told me. You've been very helpful, thank you." She got up from the table, clasped Daniel's hand and gave Abelina a quick hug.

As she hurried to her car, Jude was met with an unwelcome sight. The young men she'd seen earlier were now clustered around the station wagon taunting Finn.

"Cut it out!" Jude yelled. "Leave him alone."

One of the men rapped on the window and Finn cowered in the front seat, trembling, lips drawn back in a fearful growl. Inside a confined area like the car, if he perceived a threat, rather than fighting back he became overly submissive – a holdover, Jude believed, from the terrifying prison of his puppyhood.

Jude shouted again, "Hey! Get away from there!"

The boldest of the three stepped forward to intercept her. "Chica, Chica," he intoned and made whistling noises through his teeth. He couldn't have been more than nineteen and was drunk, that much was clear; the sweet, yeasty smell of cheap beer preceded him. "You want some, baby?" He made humping moves while he grabbed his crotch and the others laughed.

"Get out of my way," said Jude, trying to get past him.

He caught her arm and swung her around to face him, thrusting his face into hers. "You want a real man, Chica? I got whatchoo want."

Jude wrested herself away from his grip. His compatriots watched with anxious anticipation; they had no idea what Finn's growl meant and it wasn't unreasonable to think the big dog might break through a window. But at that moment a pair of headlights drew up behind Jude. The boys squinted into the bright beams. A man got out and stepped in front of the lights, his silhouette creating a shadow over the group.

"Get lost, Rodrigo," he barked to the kid who had grabbed Jude. "You too, Torres."

Jude recognized his voice. Apparently so did the three boys because they backed off and slunk away. Emmet waited until they disappeared into the darkness and then leaned against the hood of his car. "Are you alright?" he asked.

Furious, she wheeled around and opened the hatchback of the car to let Finn out. He leapt down and now free, his courage returned. He sniffed Jude first to make sure she was safe, then ran to the spot he'd last seen the three encroachers, barking out a warning that if they dared return he would take them on.

"What are you doing here?" Jude demanded.

"You're welcome," said Emmet.

"I asked you, what are you doing here?"

"And I'd ask you the same thing."

"That's really none of your business." At a standoff, they stood glaring at one another. Finally, Jude jingled her car keys and said curtly, "You're blocking me in."

"I'll move as soon as you tell me why you're here," responded Emmet.

She squared her shoulders. "Did you follow me?" she wanted to know. "Is this about Caroline?"

"No, I didn't follow you, and no, it's not about Caroline. I heard you showed up here and I've got instructions to keep employees at the plant from talking to you."

"So you've mentioned." Jude didn't know if one of the three boys had made the call – or another pair of eyes had seen her at Daniel's trailer. It seemed like there were eyes on her wherever she went. Meanwhile, Finn had come over to check out Emmet, who put out a reassuring hand to scratch him behind the ears.

"Who'd you talk to?" asked Emmet. He nodded in the direction of Daniel's trailer. "Was it Daniel Vargas?"

"Is that what your informant told you?"

"Listen, Miss Brannock, we could do this answering a question with a question thing all night, so I'll get to the point. You're not doing anybody any favors by snooping around. Trust me when I tell you that no one in Bragg Falls wants you here."

"That has already been communicated, thank you very much. Today, someone spray painted my car and poured blood all over it. Nice town."

"That's not right, but ... the reality is D&M is the only thing in Bragg Falls keeping us above water."

Jude felt uncharacteristically petulant. "Well, having heard about what's going on at the plant, maybe drowning would be the best thing."

"Look, no one at D&M is supposed to talk to you or any of your animal rights friends. And if somebody breaks rank, they're gonna get fired and they won't get another job at any Marshfield location. Then *somebody* ... like Daniel Vargas and his wife ... have no job, no income. They're back in Mexico living on the street. Is that what you want?"

She drew deep from her reserves of patience. "What I want," she answered evenly, "is to prevent animals from suffering the kind of brutality that we would never accept were they not animals raised for food. It's bad enough that the pigs you slaughter live their entire lives indoors in filthy pens or metal crates where they cannot even turn around. You've got people beating these scared animals with pipes, sticking electric prods into their eyes and mouths. Just today a downer hog was chained to a forklift and dragged across the ground. The poor animal was in agony."

Emmet rubbed an uncomfortable hand across his mouth and said gruffly, "I suppose Daniel Vargas told you that."

"Are you telling me those things *don't* happen at D&M?" challenged Jude, refusing to be trapped.

"We conform to industry standards," he said stiffly.

"Which if most people were aware of, they would find abominable. Your friend Frank Marino knew that." For the first time Jude saw doubt cross Emmet's face. She had been wondering how much he knew when he had blurted out, *I know about Frank contacting you, and I know about the videotape ... if he really did make one.* Did he in fact learn about the video from Frank or from someone else? She hadn't told anyone except Verna ... and Daniel, just now. Jude jumped in with both feet and asked, "What happened to his video? Did Bob Warshauer get it from him or is he still looking? Because I guess D&M would do just about anything to keep Frank from giving it to me."

"What the hell is that supposed to mean?" Emmet challenged.

"I find it pretty coincidental that your friend died just days after contacting our organization."

"Whoa, lady," said Emmet. "It's one thing to be an animal lover, it's another to be a paranoid militant. You're giving yourself far too much credit. Frank committed suicide. That's what the evidence says, that's all there is to it, and if you go around preaching anything to the contrary you're gonna be in a world of trouble."

He seemed more flustered than angry, yet Jude instantly regretted blurting out her suspicions. She had assumed the friendship between him and Frank went deeper than his loyalty to Marsh-field. But on second thought, that idea was naive, and she had to admit that she didn't know anything about Emmet Chapel. She steadfastly maintained eye contact and said, "Well, just for the record, no one has told me anything tonight about D&M that I didn't already know, so I trust there won't be any recrimination. There are federal protections for whistleblowers, you know."

It was a bluff – whistleblower protection for a private compa-ny employee like Daniel Vargas was a long shot. Emmet Chapel probably didn't know that, although with the smile that began to play around his mouth, she couldn't be sure.

"I'll remember that, Miss Brannock."

"And don't call me *Miss Brannock* or *Lady*. My name's Jude."

"Jude. As I recall from my Catholic education, the patron saint of lost causes." The half smile broke into a grin.

She wrenched open the Subaru hatchback and motioned for Finn to jump in, then threw over her shoulder, "We'll see about that."

CHAPTER 16

Verna Marino had rarely felt this helpless and angry. Her chapped hands shook as she rinsed the last of the dishes and placed them in the drainer in the church kitchen. A few of the other ladies from Bible study were chatting as they cleaned up. It had been a week since she lost her husband and her finances were in desperate shape, yet they went on and on about their meaningless recipes and disagreements about the placement of the church flowers. She wiped her hands on a towel and tried to shake off her un-Christian attitude. After all, the group had been very kind in the aftermath of Frank's death; she couldn't expect them to mourn with her indefinitely.

Besides, what was really bothering her was Patty Warshauer. Verna caught sight of her getting ready to leave. She had to say something.

"Patty, wait a minute," called out Verna. "I need to talk to you."

Her friend hesitated, then accompanied Verna into the refectory away from the other women. "Bob is waiting for me," said Patty impatiently.

"Why the cold shoulder tonight?" asked Verna.

Patty opened her mouth to protest, but Verna interrupted, "Please, did I do something to make you angry? Because if I did, I apologize. But don't think you're sparing my feelings by not saying what's on your mind. Honestly, it hurts worse to get the silent treatment."

Heaving a pained sigh, Patty looked first at the ceiling and then capitulated. "Bob told me that Frank was filming operations at the plant and he was going to turn the film over to some animal rights group. If you must know, we feel ... betrayed."

"I had no idea, Patty," Verna insisted.

"Really? I didn't think Frank kept any secrets from you."

"Well, obviously he did, because I knew nothing about it."

Patty pressed her lips together in disapproval. "Verna, I'm sorry for your loss, you know I am. But there are a lot of people in this town who need D&M jobs. And behind everyone's back, Frank calls some animal rights activist who breezes in to try and shut down the plant. What do those people know? These young, ho-ity-toity yuppies from Washington who think they know what's right and wrong. We are a community here."

"He meant no harm to anyone, he was just–"

"He was spying on us!"

Verna bristled at her friend's self-righteous scorn. "Well, if he was ... he was just trying to do the right thing. You've never worked inside the plant – I have. And what is happening to the animals is not very Christian, in my view."

"Then re-read your Genesis, my dear. 'Every moving thing that liveth shall be meat for you; even as the green herb have I given...'"

"That doesn't give us the right to abuse them."

The refectory door opened, letting in a burst of manure-scented air. "Oh, there you are, Verna, I was looking for you." It was

Bob Warshauer. He strolled over and put an arm around his wife. "Did you girls have a nice time tonight? Say, Patty told me about Frank's insurance policy. I am so sorry. I'm sure he didn't think about that before..." He gave his wife's shoulders an affectionate squeeze as they exchanged a sympathetic glance. "But I'm glad you're here. The company feels a responsibility to his family. So I spoke with corporate and they want to grant you six months of Frank's pay as a way to recognize his many years with Marshfield."

Verna tried to read his expression. What was Warshauer up to?

"I had to pull a few strings, so I was wondering if you'd do us a favor," he was saying. "Don't talk to Jude Brannock anymore. She's only here to cause trouble, and we really don't need any more trouble, do we?"

There was no negotiation behind Warshauer's gaze. Perhaps a warning, but most certainly a payoff for her silence – just the kind of thing Frank would have thrown back in his face. But her husband had chosen to leave life's decision-making to her, hadn't he?

"Thank you, Bob," said Verna. "That's very kind. And not to worry, there won't be any trouble from our end."

* * *

Jude got back to the motel around nine. She turned off the ignition and sat in the car, listening to the ticking of the motor as it cooled; the last thing she wanted to do was to go inside. It wasn't just that the Lysol-sprayed bathroom and cigarette-stained carpet reeked of loneliness, it was also that more work awaited her. She still had to make some notes on her conversation with the Vargases while it was fresh in her mind. Every waking minute that she documented animal torture meant navigating a thin line. On one side was the emotional connection with animals that fueled her passion, on the other side was the work ethic that often required her to turn that emotion off just to continue functioning in the face of so much pain. There were times she wondered how much longer she could walk that line.

Shaking off the self-pity, she got out of the car and opened the back for Finn. The anemic light over her motel room door had gone out, so she fumbled in her backpack for the key. But it turned out she didn't need it because the door was partially open. Jude froze and listened for any sound coming from within, then pushed against the door and let it swing open. She reached in to feel along the inside wall for the light switch.

Oh God. The room had been trashed: the covers stripped from the bed, drawers opened and the contents deposited on the floor. Jude stood surveying the chaos while Finn took his own inventory, sniffing suspiciously around the room. Right away Jude found that they'd taken her laptop and the camera, the two most valuable items. She tried to think of anything on the computer that might be damaging to the organization or to any witnesses. Luckily, she hadn't yet transcribed her interview with Daniel and Abelina, and no one else, she thought wryly, was talking. There wouldn't be much in any event. For this very reason, she brought a "clean" laptop on each new assignment. CJ was adamant about transferring or deleting files to ensure the investigators did not carry around any unnecessary information. The loss of the camera, however, was infuriating; it contained the downer photos and was even more expensive than the computer.

Cursing under her breath, Jude began the tedious task of putting things right; she folded her clothes and put them back in the drawers and cleaned up the bathroom, which had also been ransacked. From the closet she retrieved her backpack and hauled it over to the bed. Still inside were her camera lenses, chargers for the computer, and an extra battery. But when she fished into a small zippered pocket for the flash drives on which she backed up her notes and photos, she found they were both gone. Jude sat down hard on the bed, fingering the straps on her backpack.

The whole picture wasn't making sense. On the surface it looked like an ordinary burglary. The intruder had gone for the computer and camera – both re-sellable pieces of equipment. But now to learn they'd also taken the flash drives, in and of themselves not worth much ... what was that about? Jude could not help but keep coming back to the video. Earlier in the evening, Emmet Chapel had let slip that he knew about it, in which case management above him probably did as well. If Marshfield suspected that Frank had somehow gotten her a copy, they'd definitely want to look on her computer and backup drives. Maybe this was the way they had done just that, making it appear to be a random break-in.

Unanswered questions kept Jude's mind reeling. Before she went to bed, she double-checked the chain on the door. Then she lay in the dark, knowing that sleep, normally hard to come by, might be almost impossible this night. What in God's name had Frank recorded? Ever since she had come to Bragg Falls she couldn't escape the doubt she felt about his death. But now the suspicion was hardening into a word that could change everything – murder – a word that lodged like a cold stone behind her eyes, lingering until morning's light seeped around the edges of the window shade.

CHAPTER 17

The County Sheriff's Office occupied a nondescript brick building about a mile outside the town center. It was marked by two flagpoles planted in the grassy strip out front, one with an American flag, the other flying the red, white and blue blocks of the state flag. Both hung limp in the motionless air.

Jude took a seat in the waiting area, as directed by Belva Hinson, the hawk-eyed administrator at the front desk, who tartly informed her that Sheriff Ward was on the phone at present. While she waited, Jude was audience to two deputies who escorted a teenager from the holding cell in the back. Still too young to shave, the boy rubbed away some snot from the peach fuzz on his upper lip and hung his head. The officers handed Belva paperwork and chatted over his head as if he were an inanimate object. Jude began to bristle at their lack of empathy when one of the deputies put a fatherly hand on the boy's shoulder and said kindly, "Come on, Romeo. Let's get you arraigned and back to your momma before lunch," reminding Jude that first impressions could be deceiving.

A few minutes later, Belva lifted the bifocals she wore on a cord around her neck and used them to point to a short hall behind her desk. "He'll see you now. But he's got to be in court in a half hour, so make it quick."

Sheriff Grady Ward sat behind his desk looking quite unlike the man on the ridge with a gun in his hand. Still well-turned out with his snowy hair and mustache neatly combed, but no uniform and no gun, today in a business suit and tie.

"Thanks for seeing me," said Jude, taking a chair on the opposite side of his desk.

Ward gave a small grunt, outwardly none too happy that he had agreed.

"Somebody broke into my hotel room last night. My camera, my computer, and a few other items were stolen," she said, getting right to the point.

"Did you file a complaint?"

"I thought I should come see you first."

"Miss Brannock, I *run* this office. If you want to file another complaint, talk to one of the deputies or tell Mrs. Hinson outside and someone will get over to the Motor Inn to take your statement."

His reference to "another complaint" ruffled Jude, as it implied that being a victim of two crimes in such close proximity was an inconvenience. Moreover, she hadn't said anything about staying at the Motor Inn. But then again, it seemed everybody in town knew. "I gather you're aware of the damage done to my car yesterday," she said.

"I am," replied Ward, his eyes shifting to a report on his desk.

"Did anything come back on the blood?"

"It's pig blood."

"No surprise there," said Jude. "You know, between what they did to my car and the break-in at the motel last night, I get the feeling that I'm not appreciated here in Bragg Falls. I understand the general antagonism, but my investigation of violations at the plant does not warrant harassment, not to mention burglary, which I presume is a felony in this state."

"And just what is the nature of your investigation?"

"Frank Marino contacted me a couple of weeks ago. He had made a videotape of the ongoing abuses to the hogs at D&M, a ton of footage, and was going to hand over the video to our organization."

"And that would be..."

"It's called The Kinship." Ward's eyes did an involuntary roll, and Jude chose to ignore it. "Frank and I spoke on a couple of occasions. He had witnessed systematic animal cruelty at the plant and was tired of management doing nothing about it."

"So did he?"

"Did he what?"

"Did he give you this alleged video?"

"No. Apparently he killed himself before he could do that."

"I detect some sarcasm, Miss Brannock. I gather you disagree with the medical examiner's conclusion?"

"I just have some questions," she sidestepped. "For instance, did anyone on your staff find a minicam or spy camera in Frank's car?" Ward stared with a look that said he had no intention of answering. "Alright, how about his computer?" Jude pursued. "I know that was in his car because I was there at the Marino house when you brought it back to Frank's wife. Frank used a minicam to take video inside the plant, and the only way to view the video would have been to upload it onto a computer."

"And your question is..."

"Did you find such a video on his computer?"

"No, I don't believe my tech person mentioned anything,"

he answered finally. "Something like that she would have pointed out."

"Are you certain?"

"Well, if what you say is true, that there was a *ton of footage,* that would be a very large file and it would have stood out like a sore thumb. I have only your claim that Marino made a video. I haven't heard anything about it, and I hear about most everything that goes on around here. Even if he did make such a recording and intended to give it to you, he can't now. So I would suggest that your business is done. You can go home."

"You have to admit the timing is pretty odd."

Irritation crept into Ward's voice. "I don't have to admit anything. You want to play Nancy Drew, go back to wherever you came from and do it there. But not in my jurisdiction." He recalled giving her precisely the same admonition in the woods the other day and muttered to himself, "Jesus, this is like déjà vu."

"So you won't reopen the investigation into Frank's death?"

"Brannock, get the hell outta here," said Ward disgustedly. "And if we catch you trespassing on D&M property or harassing the workers, I'll lock you up."

* * *

One of the hanging bodies twisted as it swung on the moving rail that pulled it further down the line. The hog had just had his carotid artery slit and a fine spray of blood hit the side of Emmet's face as he passed. He swore out loud and lifted his arm, smearing the sweat and blood from his cheek. The sticker didn't notice and wouldn't have heard him over the din anyway; he was drenched in blood from his thick apron down to his plastic covered boots and was on to the next one. It only reminded Emmet of how glad he was that he didn't have to stick hogs for a living anymore. He'd hoped that becoming a supervisor would have kept him away from the kill floor, but it seemed like he was always down here, one problem after another. His boots tacky on the red concrete, he made his way past the stun station, where the new Hispanic guy was struggling with the tongs.

Today's nightmare, thought Emmet. *I gotta get Vernon back in the box.* Only yesterday, he'd reassigned Tim Vernon to the loading pens. Complaints had come in that the long-time stunner was toying with the equipment and threatening to electrocute anyone who looked cross-eyed at him. The others were scared of him. *And rightly so.* Emmet didn't know how much longer the guy could even stay employed; Vernon's wire thin composure was stretched to the breaking point. But his replacement wasn't handling the job and had already asked to be moved. It took a certain type of sociopath to drop forty-six hundred hogs a day.

As he headed out to the pens, Emmet heard a couple of the men whistle and from the corner of his eye saw a few quick hand movements. He knew what some of the signals meant and could count on the fact that right now metal pipes were getting kicked under the walls of the chute, electric prods getting holstered. *Don't know what you're talking about, ain't no USDA violations here.* As many years as he had been working with these guys, however, Emmet still didn't understand all the signals. The Latinos worked better if they were kept together and they'd developed a kind of unspoken language between them. Sometimes it was the barest movement of a head that told the other workers who was coming onto the floor or what was happening at the other end of the line. And the damndest thing was, it seemed to be a universal language. Hell, they had about ninety percent turnover a year. Guys quitting, new ones coming in all the time – and no matter where they came from they *all* knew the code. Sure enough, when Emmet looked behind him, he saw an inspector not far behind.

At the head of the chute, the men had gotten the message that Emmet was on his way, and they weren't happy. They were trying to move the hogs along with just their hands and plastic paddles. It wasn't easy. There was one balking at the entrance, holding up everything. Emmet barked out a command for someone to get him moving and in response, Vernon whipped out an electric prod and jammed it into the hog's rear end. The pig screamed and leapt forward, barreling into the one in front of him.

"Goddamn it, Vernon," shouted Emmet. "Put that away!"

Vernon grinned back at him, a wild look in his eyes.

"What are you going to do, Chapel, write him up?" This from the kid known as Crank, who had walked up next to him. "If we don't use the prods, we don't get 'em set up fast enough, and if we do use the prods, we get written up," he complained. "It's fucked."

"Just do the best you can," said Emmet.

"Best don't cut it," complained Crank. "Warshauer was by earlier and reamed us good."

"What'd he say?"

"He's screaming at us that the Mexicans down the line are waiting around with their thumbs up their asses."

A few of Crank's fellow workers grumbled their agreement, giving the kid courage. He stepped up in Emmet's face. "We can't fuckin' keep up and if you won't do something about it, we will."

"Oh, yeah?" responded Emmet angrily. "What are you gonna do?"

"I don't know, maybe we'll talk to the animal rights lady."

"Then you're lookin' for another job."

"Word's getting around, you know. I hear she come down here on account of Marino. At least he was trying to do something."

"No one talks to her, Crank. This is D&M business, and D&M pays your rent, your gas money, and your drugs. You know damn well you won't get anything else around here that pays a decent wage."

"Decent? You call eleven bucks an hour *decent*? And we get nuthin' unless the chain's running. If the inspectors shut it down, we stand around and don't get paid squat!"

The muscles over Emmet's cheekbones clenched. "I can't change that. You don't like it, leave."

"Just might, Chapel. I thought maybe you was gonna actually give a crap like Marino did, but you're just another one of Warshauer's whores."

Emmet spun on his heels and walked away to keep from hauling off and decking the kid. But for the rest of the morning, his hands twitched with a need to make contact with something hard.

At noon, he steered clear of the parking lot where most of the men ate their lunch and instead went to the separate break room for management. Patrick LaBrie was at a table near the vending machine eating some kind of instant soup he'd heated in the microwave. Emmet pulled out the paper bag meal that Alice had prepared – a bologna sandwich, a bag of tortilla chips and an apple.

He worked on his sandwich in silence, then tore open the bag of chips with his teeth and commented, "Warshauer's been driving the line pretty hard today."

"Uh yunh," mumbled LaBrie.

"Out in loading, they're using the prods and making the hogs jumpy. You know, Pat, we can do, like, eight or nine a minute, but it gets going faster'n that and it causes big problems inside on the kill floor."

LaBrie didn't even look up from his soup.

"You ought to come by and take a look," suggested Emmet.

"That's not my job, Chapel."

"The hell it isn't. You're USDA, it's your job to make sure there's compliance with The Humane Slaughter Act."

Waving him off with his plastic spoon, LaBrie said, "Don't start with me, Emmet. I'm on the other side the building looking at organs. I can't leave my station."

"Then send one of the other inspectors, and for Christ's sake, don't announce it ahead of time."

"I don't tell anyone else what to do."

"Jesus, Pat. There's shit goin' on over there."

"I don't want to hear about it," said LaBrie, closing his eyes behind his big glasses.

"Well, somebody's got to do something. And if I start writing up violations that go in their file, I can't get the men to work with me," said Emmet, exasperated.

"Bullshit," said LaBrie, wiping his mouth. "If you start writing up violations, Warshauer will fire your ass. That's what's bothering you."

"Well, what am I supposed to do? I got a scared kid stunning the hogs because I had to take that psycho Vernon out and put him in loading, and now he's out there ramming prods up the hogs' asses. It's not right."

"Talk to Cimino."

Emmet said hotly, "Cimino's useless. He just wants to lay low until he retires with a big ole pension. Asking him to do something is like pissing in the wind. He never comes out to lairage to look at sick hogs, and he says he doesn't control what happens on the kill floor. He's a vet, for Christ's sake, but he doesn't give a crap about the animals."

"I don't know what to tell you," said LaBrie stiffly, getting up to clear his place. "I have to get back to work. We're all just trying to survive, you know?"

Emmet had a reply on the tip of his tongue, but when he looked up, Lawrence Cimino was standing in the doorway. Tension crackled between them as it became clear that the senior USDA man had overheard the last of the conversation. Emmet dumped the rest of his lunch in the garbage before brushing past him.

Throughout the afternoon, Emmet's frustration built. There were no major mishaps, but the sight and sound of the hog screaming when Vernon jammed him ... for some reason that stayed with him. The plain truth was that animals were being abused – beaten, prodded, stabbed – just to *get* them to slaughter. He kept picturing Jude Brannock and the way she squared off against him at the trailer park, the angle of her chin catching in his headlights, her eyes alight with a fierce determination to fight for something she believed in. But that image, however alluring, also reminded him of her purpose here in Bragg Falls. If Brannock got hold of proof of what was happening at the plant, he could lose his job. His car needed a new transmission, and just yesterday, he'd written a check for Caroline's meds, which meant they'd have to shut off the cable TV and Will wouldn't be able to watch his favorite shows.

LaBrie was right. The name of the game was survival and Brannock was putting everything he had worked for in jeopardy. The truth might be plain to see, but it wasn't a simple truth.

By quitting time, the pressure on the floor had given Emmet a brutal headache and the pint of vodka in his glove compartment was the only release valve he had. Sometimes after work, he and Frank would sit in the parking lot at the Lazy Cat and finish off a bottle in the car before they ever went inside. Frank preferred his Jim Beam, but Emmet was convinced that vodka was less obvious on his breath when he got home. As the last of the day shift exited, he unscrewed the cap and with the bottle still in the paper bag, he drank deeply. The alcohol was smooth going down his throat, then followed with its comforting burn. He took another swallow and waited for the buzz, the release, the anesthesia that would deaden the pain.

He was down to a third of a bottle and still hadn't started the car when he heard tapping on the driver's window. He looked up and saw a familiar face.

"You're Caroline's dad, right?" asked the man.

Emmet slowly got out of the car. "Yeah, hi..."

"Vince Guarino. My daughter Rosie goes to school with Caroline."

"Oh sure," said Emmet. As he stood up, feeling the full brunt of the vodka, he had a vague memory of sitting next to Guarino at a track meet the year before.

"I just got a job on the cleaning crew," said Vince. "My wife got laid off and I figured I could pull in a little extra income ... working a second job at night."

"Well, uh, glad it fits your schedule."

"So, your family's well?"

"Yup, and you?"

"Good, good. How's your daughter doing in school? Junior year's a tough one."

"She's fine." Emmet forced a chuckle. "Could improve her grades some."

"Tell me about it."

Warming slightly to a fellow parent with a seemingly underachieving child, Emmet said, "Yeah, she could get straight A's if she wanted, but she's lazy. The only thing she seems interested in is her Italian class."

"Italian?"

"Yeah, she's taking first year Italian. Always lugging around her text book and talking to her little brother in Italian."

Guarino frowned. "Maybe you mean Spanish? Because they don't teach Italian at the high school."

CHAPTER 18

Caroline sat cross-legged on the floor, her back against the bed, her headphones clamped to her ears to keep her mom and younger brother at a distance. The music and the book in her hands were transporting her to another place and time. She got the travel book from the school library because of its vivid color photographs of Italy. She lingered at one particular picture – an early evening at the Piazza de Spagna in Rome. The sky was a silky blue and a gold, setting sun shone on a crowd of young people who milled about the steps of the Trinità dei Monti church. The scene was vibrant, yet peaceful, and even though the anti-anxiety medication was making Caroline nauseous, a sweet warmth moved through her as she pictured herself sitting on those same steps. In her imagination, her hair was grown out, long and luxurious; she wore a string of fake pearls and a flowing white skirt. She was sitting next to a handsome, funny Italian boy and they were laughing. Matteo maybe, or Bertrando. He was one of the group of friends she'd made in that glorious summer – the last summer.

The fantasy dissolved, as it invariably did, into the final scene. This time she was floating face down in the murky water of a canal, her skirt billowing out around her like a sail. Her friends clung to one another and wept on the embankment. Caroline closed her eyes and tried to feel what it would be like to be dead. Could she see what her friends were doing? Her parents? Would she be lonely?

Without warning, her father burst into the room, bringing with him the heat of fury. Her guard should have been up right away, but the medication had made her foggy; she merely raised her eyes without taking off her headphones.

"I swear to God, you will not lie to me again, Caroline," he growled.

"What?" she asked, her mouth dry.

"Take those things off!"

Oh yeah. He hated when she kept her earplugs in when he was talking. She pulled them out of her ears and the present came back into focus. "What is it now?" she asked.

"Your Italian *course*," he said darkly. "The one that takes all your time from your other work."

"Oh." She paled.

"You lied to me and you lied to your mother."

"Well, I don't think I actually told you–"

"Goddamn it, Caroline. You told us that you were studying Italian in school, and now I find out that they don't teach Italian. Meanwhile, your other grades are going down the toilet. What the hell is going on?"

"I'm not going to fail anything, Dad," she said peevishly.

"Don't take that tone with me. According to your last report card, you're damn close. You don't get it. Life is hard. It's not some gondola trip in Venice. It's time you shape up, young lady."

"I'm not going to fail. Get a life, Dad."

His daughter's petulance made Emmet angrier. He strode the few short steps across the room and snatched the book from her hand. "I'm sick to death of your lies and your morbid fantasies," he snapped.

It was as if he had struck her.

"You call *me* morbid? What about you? You kill pigs all day and come home reeking of blood and guts."

"It pays for the roof over your head and the food on your table," fumed Emmet.

Caroline thrust out her chin. "And is that the kind of life I have to look forward to? Live in Bragg Falls like you and eat fucking Hamburger Helper every night? If I work really hard, is that what I get? I get to work in a hellhole like you?"

Emmet pulled his hand back to slap her across the face. But he couldn't do it. With no other place for his fury to go, in one quick motion he ripped the travel book in half. Caroline gasped.

"Don't ... ever ... lie to me ... again," he said, tossing the mutilated book into the corner. He wheeled around and stormed out of the room.

Caroline crawled over to the book and tried to piece the two ragged halves together with trembling hands. Desolate tears fell on the happy tourists of the Piazza De Spagna, and where each tear landed, a tiny buckle appeared on the paper until the photo was unrecognizable.

* * *

When Jude arrived at the Lazy Cat, a small cluster of men hanging around the entrance were watching the red bubble lights of a Deputy Sheriff's car pull out of the driveway and disappear down the road. Whatever had happened to warrant the arrival of the cops, however, seemed to give rise to more amusement than distress. The men parted to let her pass and she overheard a few of them still laughing about the incident as they got in their cars to go home.

Tonight she'd decided to take another crack at the Lazy Cat where alcohol might loosen some tongues. But the place was nearly empty. A few half-filled glasses sat abandoned on tables and the music was barely audible. Howard Bisbee was at the bar, examining his arm and dabbing at it with a wet cloth smeared with blood. The bartender, Nick, was on a hunt for a first aid kit.

Jude walked over towards Bisbee and saw a nasty red slice running across his forearm. "What happened here?" she asked, frowning.

Bisbee glanced at her, but didn't respond. The first aid box appeared on the bar and Nick began to scavenge its contents. "Just your ordinary bar fight," he said. "Some drunk says the wrong thing to a paranoid moron with a hunting knife. Happens all the time."

"Oh, dear," exclaimed Jude, then with a half smile turned to Bisbee. "Were you the drunk or the paranoid moron?"

"Neither," he informed her.

"I've been expecting this for a while," said Nick. "Vernon is a walking IED and I hope they lock his ass up for a long time. You going to press charges?"

"No," said Bisbee.

Nick produced some gauze along with a roll of surgical tape and began to peel off a long strip. He looked around for a way to cut the tape and as he did, it became stuck to itself in several places.

Jude said, "Here, let me do that." She took the stool next to Bisbee, who hesitated for a moment before surrendering his arm. "You probably could use some stitches," she advised.

"I've had worse. It'll heal up."

"Your call." Jude pulled the first aid kit over and found a tube of antibiotic ointment. She dressed Bisbee's wound, tearing the sticky tape expertly with her teeth and using it to hold the gauze in place.

Nick leaned on the bar and watched. "You're lucky he didn't cut off a couple of fingers," he commented. "That's one big knife Vernon was whipping around. I sure wouldn't have gotten in the middle."

"I'm used to knives," Bisbee shrugged.

"Guess working at D&M will do that for you," Nick commented.

"The first thing you learn there is the value of a good knife."

"Yeah, what's the second thing?"

"You don't want to work with a knife."

Jude smoothed the last piece of tape over the gauze. "There, that ought to hold you."

Meanwhile, Nick had disappeared into the back. He came out with three long neck beers, popped the tops, and slid two of them down the counter to Bisbee and Jude. Then he lifted his own. "Cheers."

While he went off to clear the tables, Jude and Bisbee drank in silence. After a moment, Bisbee lifted his bandaged arm in acknowledgment. "Thank you," he said.

"You're welcome."

"No talking about D&M, okay?"

"I wasn't even going to ask," Jude smiled. "We'll talk about something else. So, where do you live?"

"Here in town," said Bisbee.

"You married?"

"No."

"Live alone?"

"No, I live with my mother." He caught himself and with a hint of amusement in his eyes, added, "Don't get the wrong impression."

"Mr. Bisbee, in my job I meet too many unusual people to stereotype anybody."

"Call me Howard."

"Okay, and I'm Jude." She held out her hand and he engulfed it in his own with a firm handshake. "Is your mother in good health?"

"For someone seventy-five and worked as hard as she did, I guess."

Jude stayed silent, inviting him to go on.

"My mom raised three kids by herself," said Bisbee proudly. "She mopped floors and cleaned toilets at the school right here in Bragg Falls for most of that time."

"Are your siblings able to help out?"

He shook his head. "My younger sister died of cancer awhile back and my brother went another way entirely. He won't get out of jail for another ten years."

"I guess that leaves you with a lot of responsibility."

"It does, but I don't mind. My mom's grandparents were sharecroppers, sons and daughters of slaves, and she still carries that with her somewhere deep. She's got a lot of pride and I'd do just about anything to keep her off public assistance."

"Which is why you stay at D&M," Jude proffered.

"That's right."

"What do you do?"

"Right now I'm a foreman, but I used to be a sticker – nine years, not all of them here. I was in Iowa for awhile."

"That's a long time on the rail."

Bisbee gazed down at her with more than a little curiosity. "You know your way around a packing plant?"

"Once, for a few weeks on the cut line. I was undercover."

Taking this last information with equanimity, Bisbee nodded. "How was that?"

"Horrible. The worst job I've ever done." Jude took a big swallow and stared at the bottle, watching a drop of condensation drip down the side. "It was a kosher slaughterhouse. They took all kinds of animals ... steer, sheep, goats. It was a much smaller operation than D&M so we were right next to the kill floor. I could hear the animals bellowing and could see them convulsing on the floor. You know, in kosher slaughter, they don't stun the animals."

"I ... I didn't know that."

"Unhunh. Where I worked, they drive the animal into this contraption that holds the body immobile with just the head sticking out. The animal is looking around, but it can't move. Then they up and cut its throat and wait for the bleed out. As that goes on, the animal collapses and drops to the floor. Sometimes it's still writhing around, choking on its own blood while they rip out the trachea and esophagus and chuck 'em in a pail. All in the name of religious ... purity, I suppose."

Normally, she tried not to recall those painful, dark days. It was the only undercover she had abandoned for emotional reasons, and the sights and sounds from that time still hunted her down in her sleep. But that was in her early years with Gordon; she had, at least in the daylight hours, toughened up since then. "Anyway..."

Bisbee was moved. He liked this girl who had tended to his wound so competently and was so straightforward. Finally, he said softly, "At D&M we try to do it humanely, but I suppose it's not much of an improvement. I mean, you know the animals suffer, and you ... you shut your emotions off. Just can't think about it."

"How do you do that?"

"Don't have to try, just happens. You spend enough time on the floor and you're killing things, one every few seconds, you develop a shield that doesn't let you care. You go dead inside. So many guys I know they can't switch it on and off like a light, and they go home to their families still weighed down by that shield, don't care about nothing. And why bother trying to fix that? You just gotta wake up next morning and do the same thing, over and over again."

Jude's eyes brimmed with tears, but the investigator in her swallowed them back. Bisbee wanted to tell someone – needed to tell someone.

She asked, "How about you, do you always carry your shield?"

"If I didn't, I think I'd go out of my mind." And with that, Bisbee drained his beer and got up. He mumbled a second thanks and offering Nick a vague salute, ambled out of the bar. Watching him go, Jude found herself wondering about the shield, the one that she was carrying with her every day.

A few minutes later, Jude headed out to her car and literally collided with Emmet, who was too busy replaying the scene he'd had with his wife to watch where he was going. Alice had seemed more wounded even than Caroline, but it didn't keep her from lashing out at him. As midnight bore down, they argued outside the house so the kids wouldn't hear. *What kind of man would be so cruel to his own daughter? I don't know you anymore, Emmet. I don't know if it's the drinking or what it is, but you're not the man I married, and I'm not sure if you're the man I want to stay married to.* He vowed an apology to his daughter in the morning; he hung his head and made a half-hearted attempt to tell Alice the kind of pressure he faced at the plant. But his fumbling explanation came out short and bitter. He resented Alice's constant fretting about the family's finances that always made him feel inadequate as a provider. *What do we do if you quit?* she demanded. *Already we can't afford a second car or to fix the boiler. We can't afford to go anywhere as a family, even to go out for dinner. Or God forbid, take a vacation.* The list of failures was too much for him. Emmet made a run for the place where he knew he could forget.

And he nearly knocked Jude over as she was coming out of the bar. For a moment they were both stunned.

Emmet took a step back, crossed his arms and said, "Oh, it's you. I would've thought you'd be back in Washington with your vegetarian friends by now."

"Yeah, it's me," replied Jude tersely, brushing herself off as a symbolic gesture. "And don't worry, I was just leaving."

She started to walk away, but he stopped her. "Where's Tonto?"

"Tonto?" She turned.

"Your furry sidekick."

"What, you think I'm the Lone Ranger?"

"Might as well be."

"For your information, I may be here in Bragg Falls by myself. But I am not alone in this. There are thousands, no, millions of people who understand that animals are beings that feel pain, have emotions, and are not just assembly-line widgets."

"Millions, hunh." Emmet turned his back and this time it was Jude who called after him.

"Do you know why the Lone Ranger used silver bullets? They were to remind him that life is precious and like his bullets, not to be wasted or thrown away."

He walked back to where she stood, her breath coming out in misty puffs. The evening had turned cold and she had on just a light jacket zipped up to her chin. The reflection of the bar's neon sign made the loose braid slung over her shoulder gleam like copper, and Emmet imagined that if he touched it, it might burn. There was that challenge in her eyes that had haunted him all day.

"Is that some kind of animal rights slogan or are you trying to tell me something?" he asked.

"Just thought if you're going to speak in innuendo, I'd do the same."

"Miss Brannock, I don't know much about you, but I do know that speaking in *innuendo* is not your style."

Jude had to smile. "You're right. I don't think it's your style, either."

"Shit, I'm not even sure what innuendo means."

At that they both laughed, and Jude was taken aback at how his diffident, easy grin transformed him, making him look boyish and approachable. They both looked down at the ground and there was an uncomfortable pause. Jude finally broke it, saying, "Well, I guess I'll see you around."

"Don't push your luck," Emmet counseled with another broad smile. But she had gone only a few steps when his resolve failed. "Don't go," he called out. "Let me ... I'll buy you a beer."

Against her better judgment, Jude walked back into the Lazy Cat, letting him hold the door for her.

Jude really didn't want another beer, but when Emmet brought two Buds over to the table, she didn't say anything, in uncharted territory as it was. She felt drawn to him and wasn't sure why. He embodied something that infuriated her more than animal cruelty itself – the stubborn, defensive unwillingness to acknowledge it. But she didn't think he was a cruel man and she latched onto the scar that cut across his cheekbone as a visible sign that whatever his activities at D&M, he had not escaped unwounded.

"Aren't you worried that someone from the plant will see us together?" she asked, although the bar was practically empty.

"I'll just say I was interrogating you."

"What do you want to know?"

He eyed her for a moment before asking, "So you think animals should have the same rights as people?"

"That's a philosophical question that quite honestly I don't spend much time on. I think that debate should take a back seat to the more immediate and ongoing calamity, which is that animals are suffering terribly and unnecessarily for the sake of our fashion, entertainment, and yes, food."

"Some folks wouldn't agree with you, or just don't care."

"Of course. But I know that many more do care and would be horrified to know, for example, how pigs are raised. The sows kept in metal crates on concrete floors their entire lives, unable to turn around or engage in a single natural behavior. These are smart, feeling creatures and the confinement drives them insane. Three-week-old piglets snatched away from their mothers and castrated and tail-docked without anesthesia, or the ones too sick to make it, body slammed against a concrete floor until they're dead ... if they're lucky ... some of them just get thrown into the garbage while they're still alive. You know as well as I do that it's all standard industry practice. But most people have no idea what's going on and that's the way Marshfield and the rest of them want to keep it."

"There are laws," protested Emmet. "Humane Slaughter Act, for one."

"Which is useless as long as it relies on profit-seeking companies to self-monitor."

"We have USDA personnel at the plant."

"Who, as much as the workers, rely on the good will of plant management to move up the ranks."

Emmet thought about the times, especially in the last few weeks, he'd seen Frank Cimino reading the newspaper in his office while hogs were getting kicked, beaten ... and worse. He passed a hand over his mouth as if to wipe away this discussion. "Didn't really want to get into that," he said. "I'd rather talk about you."

"Well, this is me. This is what I care about."

"And being you is a full time job, eh?"

"Pretty much."

"You have a family?' he asked, glancing at her left hand for a ring.

"Not the kind most people have," Jude replied. "And no, I'm not married."

"Parents?"

"None that would matter." Registering his surprise at her curt answer, she echoed, "Didn't really want to get into that. Suffice it to say, I was a ward of New York State."

"Sorry."

"It's all right. I learned quite a bit about life during that time."

"Is that how you got to be so tough?"

"I'm not that tough, trust me."

"But you're very single minded," said Emmet, looking at her curiously. "We don't see eye to eye on this animal thing, but you're passionate about it. You've got a dream, a commitment, and I ... I admire that."

Jude lifted her eyebrows. "Don't you? Have a dream, I mean?" When he took refuge in his beer, she pressed, "Seriously, if you weren't working at D&M, what would you be doing? What would you *want* to do?"

"I don't know..." He looked decidedly ill at ease with the question. But Jude drew her foot up to her seat, clasping her knee with her hands, and settled back to let him know that she wasn't going anywhere until she had an answer.

He drew in a long breath. "I suppose I'd work for myself," he said. "I'm pretty good with my hands. Me and Frank did his whole roof a few years back. I started out as a carpenter's apprentice."

She could see it. His hands were strong with long fingers – competent hands that could build things and fix them if they broke.

"Why'd you stop?"

Emmet chuckled, "You're relentless, you know that? Damn, you remind me of Caroline ... I'll tell you a story about her. When I was still doing carpentry, one day she begs me to teach her how to hammer. She was *six years old*. Over my wife's objections, I set her up with some boards, nails and a hammer and showed her how." Tenderness softened the lines around his eyes as he remembered. "She was this tiny thing with a pony-tail; I remember she had on a yellow t-shirt with pictures of fish on it. She marches out with this fierce expression on her face and goes at it with that hammer. Like, *Grrr.* And she'd get so mad when the nails bent over, but she never gives up. After awhile I pop a beer, sit back and watch. She was so determined. Kind of like you, I think."

"I'll take that as a compliment, but you didn't answer my question. Why did you stop carpentry-ing?"

"Money, what else?" said Emmet, shifting in his seat. "The work wasn't steady, and I had a wife and kid to think about. Caroline was starting school and we were trying to have another baby... We can't all follow our passion, you know."

"Maybe not. But whatever you're doing, you can stand up and fight for what's decent and moral."

A weary sadness came over him. "It's easy for you to say. I try to speak up, but there's only so much you can do. Look at Frank, he was always fighting with management and all it did was crush him. Toe the line with Warshauer and still keep the respect of the guys on the floor, it'll squeeze you so bad you can't breathe." He looked at her evenly for a moment. "Maybe you think we enjoy hurting animals. Okay, every once in a while you get some crazy like Tim Vernon, but most of us don't want the hogs to suffer. We don't have the tools or the time to do it any different. If Marshfield wants to make a profit, they've got to hit the numbers – turn out so many head every day, keep up with the competition. Managers like me have to keep the line moving to do what the big bosses want, and the men on the floor have to do whatever it takes to keep the managers happy. That's just the way it is. And I'll be honest with you, I've done some bad things myself to those hogs."

Jude let his confession hang between them for a moment. She'd felt compassion towards Bisbee, but didn't want to let Emmet off the hook and wasn't sure why. Finally she asked, "Are you looking for forgiveness?"

Emmet put his elbows on the table and his head in his hands. "I don't know, but I get the feeling I'm not gonna get it from *you*."

"It's not mine to give," she said. In an effort to keep him engaged she put her hand lightly on his arm. Quickly she pulled it back, knowing they both felt it more intensely than the single touch of encouragement she'd intended. "Change is always possible," she went on. "And the first thing is to tell the truth, let customers see what's really going on at D&M so they can decide if that's what they want. I happen to believe that if people knew, most of them wouldn't stand for it. Frank also believed that; that's why he made the tape."

Looking up bleary-eyed, Emmet was torn. He wanted an end to this conversation, but more, he wanted the feel of her hand on his skin again.

"You were his best friend," said Jude. "You must have known something about it."

"Have you heard a word I said?" asked Emmet, digging in a back pocket for his wallet, along with the courage to push her away. "I don't know about what Frank did and I don't want to know. I've got a family and bills to pay. Besides, it's too late. I grew up in this town. My parents are buried in the same cemetery as Frank. My whole life is here, and I don't have any choice but to ride it out. Don't you know by now? Nothing stops the chain."

CHAPTER 19

Carpeting soaked up the murmuring voices and the clink of silverware in the executive dining room. Seldon Marshfield and Richard Hillman sat away from the others at the CEO's reserved table overlooking the sculpture garden where the midday sun played on modernistic granite forms.

"How's the sole today, Jimmy?" asked Marshfield, perusing the leather-bound menu.

"Very fresh today, sir. I would recommend it," answered the waiter.

"Then that's what I'll have." With a broad smile, Marshfield patted his stomach. "Nothing to start. I'm watching my weight."

Because he didn't want to take up his boss's time ordering a more extensive meal, Hillman said he'd have the same. But he knew a little piece of fish wouldn't satisfy and dug into the bread basket as the waiter took their menus.

Marshfield checked his watch, then asked, "What do you hear from our friend in Bucharest?"

"It's all taken care of," replied Hillman. "He knows someone who works directly with the Minister of Agriculture and says he can get quick approval for the new facility in Prahova. The environmental regulations won't slow our expansion."

"How much is this going to cost?"

"Two hundred thousand."

"Fine. Launder it however you think best. And what about Bragg Falls?"

On this subject Hillman was less confident, but tried not to let it show. "All in all, that's going as planned. The girl doesn't appear to have a copy of the tape. My guy, who has good tech skills, checked her computer, backup materials and handwritten notes. He made it look like a routine burglary at her hotel room."

"I don't understand why she's still hanging around," said Marshfield with a frown.

"She won't for long," assured Hillman. "No one is talking to her and we've got some pushback building in the community."

"We don't have time for that, Dick. I want the situation in Bragg Falls wrapped up quickly. I'm talking *yesterday*. In a few days the State Senate is going to pass the re-vamped Agriculture Terrorism Bill." He shook out his napkin with great satisfaction. "The taking of unauthorized photographs or video at any agricultural facility will carry jail time. So will any distribution of the recordings, which is going to shut down these animal rights groups."

Hillman was surprised. "I thought it was dead in committee."

"Nope. Quite alive and approved by the Judiciary Committee."

"What about Senator Gilbert? I thought he was holding it up."

"Arnie Gilbert?" Marshfield dismissed the man with a flick of his hand. "Arnie is up for re-election. We gave nearly seventy-five thousand to his campaign."

"I thought he had a pretty big bankroll himself."

"Since when has it ever been enough?" chastised Seldon.

Hillman grunted a concession and helped himself to another roll.

"More persuasive, however, I secured him a seat on our Task Force at the Council," said Marshfield, referring to the American Legislative Exchange Council, known as ALEC, a corporate funded group that crafted pro-business bills for state and federal legislators. "Now he can have a bigger hand in writing the medical tort reform he's so keen on."

"I heard a few corporations have bailed on ALEC. They don't like some of the bad publicity that's brewing."

Marshfield scrutinized his security director for signs that he knew more than he should. At the highest levels of corporate protection, in the shadows behind ALEC, only a handful of men made the rules. Seldon Marshfield was one of them; not even Hillman could have access. The CEO chose to ignore the comment and put Hillman back on defense. "A few more days we'll be home free. Just get that animal lady out of there and make sure that tape never surfaces. Whatever you have to do."

* * *

Jude looked up at the sign: Five Star Body 'n Paint. In the open garage, a young man in a paint splattered uniform was taping a sheet of plastic over the windshield of a sedan. A respirator mask, held in place with a rubber strap, had been pushed to the top of his afro.

"Excuse me, are you the owner?" asked Jude.

The young man grinned. "Just the hired man. Want me to git Mr. Clay for ya?"

"No bother, I'll find him."

She didn't have to since the owner, a red-faced, jowly man in his fifties, strolled out from the office. "Afternoon, how ya'll doin' today?" he asked like a man who wanted to do business.

"Not bad. I saw your ad in the paper and wanted to swing by and get an estimate," said Jude.

"How about we take a look see, then. Where you parked?"

Jude walked him over to the Subaru, which she had left in the semi-shade of a thatch of mimosa trees whose leaves were covered in a light film of spray paint. The first thing Mr. Clay noticed was Finn's large head sticking out the passenger window.

"He's a big fella," he said. "Friendly?" Before Jude could answer, he exclaimed, "Fer cryin' out loud!" He'd seen the writing on the car. "Who did that?"

"I don't know," said Jude.

Clay turned his head sideways to read it. "Your turn ... son?" he queried.

Jude sighed. "I hope I don't have to get the whole car repainted."

He assessed the damage, closing one eye first, then the other. "We could do just the doors, but I can't guarantee an exact match on the color. Might be better off with the full job, ma'am."

"I'll stick with just the doors. How soon could you do it?"

"We're finishin' up a couple tomorrow. Could get to it on Thursday."

"Now the hard part," said Jude. "How much?"

Clay chortled, "Bless yer heart. Don't you worry, we'll work out somethin' for your budget. Why'nt you come inside and we kin write it up."

He headed back to the office and Jude followed, working on an addition problem: this month's rent plus her Visa bill, and now the cost of this paint job.

Five minutes later, estimate in hand, she crossed the front lot and saw the empty Subaru.

"Finn?" Jude felt the icy nails of fear rake down her back. "Finn?!"

The car was as she had left it, but he was gone. How was that possible? She'd only been inside the office for a few minutes and he couldn't have gotten out ... the window opening was too small.

"Finn! Here, boy. Come on, boy!" She whistled. Then called again and again. Anger crept into her voice in hopes that he was nearby and simply not responding. She ran to the area behind the auto body shop, then back to the road, praying she wouldn't find him hit by a car. By this time, the shop owner and his young worker had come out to see about the commotion. Clay scratched his head and offered a couple of implausible scenarios: Finn had squeezed out the window or someone had happened by and fearing the dog was hot inside, let him out. But Jude knew that if he had gotten out he would have come looking for her.

Clay's young worker finally said, "Maybe somebody took him."

She had begun to believe that was the only explanation, but his words knocked the breath right out of her.

CHAPTER 20

Sheriff Ward wasn't the only one with a sense of déjà vu. Jude could hardly believe that she was here again at headquarters filing her third complaint in as many days. Belva Hinson had her complete a short form and was sympathetic, having two Scottish Terriers of her own. But she explained that the department could not devote resources to finding a lost dog. "They usually turn up," she said. Jude tried to explain that he wasn't lost, that someone *took* Finn and that it was connected to the vandalism of her car and the break-in at her hotel room. Hinson would only go so far as to admit it might have been a "prank" and reasserted her belief from long experience that Finn would turn up.

As long as she was doing something, Jude was able to keep from imagining all the terrible things that could have happened to him. As she searched along the road where the auto body shop was located, a mile in each direction, she kept expecting Finn to come bounding around the corner at any moment. Every movement caught her eye and she'd stop and wait ... just in case. In town she went into every storefront and asked, "Have you seen my dog?" In many blank faces she could see that it was as though she had inquired about a lost wallet or set of keys. They didn't understand that Finn was a piece of her heart. Her best friend, her rock, her protector. Jude sometimes had to struggle to keep him from becoming a human surrogate – she respected his animalness too much. And he rewarded her not just with unconditional love and loyalty, but by being a living reminder of the ability of animals to feel pain, fear, and joy. Finn was everything that steadied and renewed her motivation to fight for all of them.

She mounted a one-woman search party, stopping off at the motel in case he had found his way back there. She made up a flyer with his photo, description, and an offer of a reward, then had copies run off at a print shop at the mall. More trouble ensued when she began to post them around town.

At the hardware and feed store, an assistant manager declined her request to pin a flyer to the bulletin board in the vestibule.

"We don't let folks do that kind of thing," he said.

"What are you talking about?" challenged Jude. "What are these?" She pointed to business cards and printed notices that offered everything from babysitting services to used cars to firewood.

He crossed his arms, revealing damp sweat stains at the armpits. "That's advertising," he proclaimed.

"So? I'm offering a reward, that's advertising."

The assistant widened his stance and reiterated his position. "No can do. Yours is different."

Jude stormed out hoping that it was just this particular fellow being difficult. But a few other establishments on the block gave her the same treatment, and although she suspected the real reason, it didn't become entirely clear until she got to Roy Mears's diner.

"Why if it ain't the animal rights lady," he said when she came through the door.

Paying no attention to his sneer, she held up a copy of the flyer. "Mr. Mears, would you mind if I taped this up?"

"Damn right, I'd mind." He turned his back on her to flip a hamburger on the grill.

"Please. This has nothing to do with the plant," Jude entreated. "This is about my missing dog. It's personal."

"I'll tell you what's personal," he shot back. "How you come here looking to put folks out of work. That's personal to me."

Letting her anger flare, Jude burst out, "I'm not looking to put anyone out of work. I came here to try and set some things right because apparently no one else really cares."

At that, Mears turned mean. He lifted the sizzling hamburger patty on his long spatula and shoved it in Jude's face. "So whiles you're waitin' on us to *really care*, how about a nice hamburger? A nice, juicy piece of cow flesh, running with blood and ripped right off its nice, fat ass."

Disgusted, Jude turned her head away and muttered, "Jerk."

Mears jabbed the spatula at her again. "I heard that. Get the fuck out of here, you terrorist bitch."

Outside on the sidewalk, she found herself shaking and had to grab hold of a parking meter to keep her legs from giving way. *Oh God, they despise me. Please, please, don't let them hurt Finn. He didn't do anything to them.*

The town's obvious hostility hurried her along on Main Street. She worked her way down one side of the street, then the other, attaching flyers to telephone poles and slipping them under the wiper blades of parked cars. It wasn't long before she felt a presence behind her. She looked back and saw a familiar figure in a camouflage cap and coveralls following her – the same man who'd mimed shooting her and Daniel Vargas the other day. He ambled behind, hands in pockets, staying half a block back. He waited across the street while she asked to post a flyer inside a few stores, and was still watching her when she went into the convenience mart at the gas station.

The woman at the counter was a relief from the cold shoulder she had been getting. In fact, not only did she say she'd take a flyer home with her and show it to her neighbors, she offered a further suggestion.

"Did you stop by the paper?" she queried.

"The paper?"

"Sure 'nuff. The *Bragg Falls Chronicle* has offices down off of Third Street, which is two blocks that'a way. There's never much happens around here, so they don't got a whole lot of news." A grin deepened the spidery lines around her eyes into creases. "Might be your missing dog is a big story. Just kidding, but maybe they can print sump'n up for you."

"Thanks. One more favor if I could." Jude looked over her shoulder and spotted the man in the cap talking to someone in a pickup truck at one of the pumps. "You have an exit out back I can use?"

If she'd been driving, she would have missed it, but on foot Jude spotted the twelve-inch plaque for the *Chronicle* mounted on the side door of what appeared to be a residential home. She pushed it open and went up the narrow staircase to the newspaper offices, housed in a couple of renovated bedrooms on the second floor.

In the front office sat Caroline's boyfriend Jack Delaney, whom she'd last seen on the ridge overlooking the plant. He was dressed in the same black t-shirt and jeans, but now his hair was pulled back from his face with a rubber band. He sat with his feet up on the desk, a sketch pad in his lap and a drawing pen in his ink-stained fingers. So engrossed in his design, he hadn't heard Jude's footsteps on the stairs.

"Jack?"

His feet swung off the desk in guilty admission, but when he saw who it was, his slumping posture let her know that he regretted this minimal show of respect.

"I'm Jude, you remember? We met in the woods the other day. You're Caroline's friend."

"Yeah."

She wasn't sure which of her statements he was acknowledging, but pressed forward. "Do you work here?"

"Yeah."

"Is the paper daily, weekly, what?"

"Why?"

"I want to put in an ad or a notice."

"Awright."

After a pause, Jude asked irritably, "Are you able to put a whole sentence together? With a subject and a verb and everything? My dog is missing and I want to get him back as quickly as possible."

Seemingly unmoved by her sarcasm, he peered at her through half-closed eyes. "Same dog you had? The one Caroline likes so much?"

"Yeah, you jealous?"

He scoffed in response.

"When is the soonest I can get an ad in?"

"The print version comes out once a week. But we do an online issue every day."

"Okay, can I get it in for tomorrow?"

Jack reluctantly put his pad on the desk and swiveled in his chair to face a computer. "If you don't care about design or fonts or anything, just tell me what you want it to say. You have a picture?"

When she handed him a flyer, he said curtly, "No, I mean digital."

"I have one on my phone. I can send it to you."

He pulled up a form on the computer and his fingers hovered over the keys. "What do you want to say? Keep it under two hundred characters."

"I guess ... lost dog, dark brown except for some light brown fur on his muzzle and over his eyes. A little bit of white on his neck and chest, and some on his legs. He has a limp, his right hind leg. Let's see ... his ears flop over. He's got a very ... noble face." Her voice cracked with emotion and she looked away in embarrassment.

"With spaces, you're over two hundred characters," Jack announced flatly.

"Fine," flashed Jude. "Just say, 'Stolen dog. Reward for return. No questions asked.' What's the matter with you, anyway? I thought you were a friend of Caroline's, or are you also part of the militia trying to run me out of town?"

Chastened by her outburst, he tapped out the text on the keys, then eyed her over his shoulder. "It's just I don't trust a lot of people."

"That makes two of us," replied Jude.

"Was he really stolen?" asked Jack in a more conciliatory tone. "Was it because of D&M ... you know, did somebody take your dog as payback because of your investigation?"

"Yes, I believe they did."

"It's a shitty thing to do," he said. "But I'm not surprised. You know, everyone in town in some way or other depends on the plant, including my dad with this paper. But for what it's worth, I think you're doing a good thing. Bragg Falls is my home and all, but well ... me and Caroline think it's a really filthy place to live, physically and morally. Last year, there was blood and pig shit and who knows what leeching into the creek, killed everything in it. Someone from the big ole United States government came down and made the plant pay a fine – the equivalent of a corporate speeding ticket. Still no fish in that creek. Can't swim there, can't even get close to it or you get sick. But somebody's making money!" Jack smiled and began to sing in soft, mocking tones, "*Oh beautiful, for spacious skies for amber waves of grain, for purple mountains–*"

The door to the next room opened and a man with Jack's build plus fifty pounds stood glowering in the doorway.

His son paled and the bravado fell away. He made as if they were in the middle of a transaction. "So, we'll put it in like an ad. That's forty-five, check or cash."

Jude pulled out her wallet, but saw she was short. "Do you take credit cards?" she asked.

Mr. Delaney answered for his son, "Not unless you have an account." The way he looked at her, Jude suspected he knew who she was. He confirmed it when he turned to Jack and asked pointedly, "Did you finish the layout on the second page? I have to get home and change. Your mom and I are having dinner with the Warshauers tonight."

Jack actually blushed at the mention of his parents' relationship with the plant manager, but he said only, "It's done, Dad."

The elder Delaney backed into his office but left the door open.

"There's an ATM about three blocks over," Jack advised.

"I know where it is. I'll be back in a few minutes," said Jude. "You'll stick around?"

"Yeah, but make it quick. As you heard, my father's in a hurry. Big dinner plans."

She raced down the steps and along the sidewalks to the bank. At the ATM, she punched in her PIN number and retrieved the cash. But as she turned to go back, she came face to face with the man in the camouflage cap. Up close, Jude could see his deeply pockmarked skin and in the curl of his lip the years of torment from his peers that had nurtured a cruel streak.

"You looking for these?" he snickered, holding up a handful of flyers that he'd ripped down from the telephone poles. "Poor baby poochie is lost?"

"Get out of my way." Jude tried to move around him, but he sidestepped in front of her. She looked around but there was no one on the street.

"You don't listen too good, do you?" he asked.

"I listen fine. I just don't respond to threats."

He backed her up with his hands on her shoulders and pressed her into the brick wall of the bank. "Yeah, well, maybe you should."

"Get your hands off me," she warned.

"Or what?" he asked. Using his forearm to hold her, he moved one hand down to her breast and stepped in to push his pelvis into hers.

Jude let him get just close enough and then rammed her knee into his groin. She ducked under his falling torso to avoid a collision as he lurched forward, dropping to his knees and grabbing at his crotch.

"Or that," she said. Then she bent down to speak directly into his ear and added, "And if anything happens to my dog, I will find you and finish the job. Do I make myself clear?"

She didn't wait for an answer. But he couldn't have given her one, not with his forehead pressed to the pavement.

Jude ran all the way back to the *Chronicle*, frightened not for herself but for Finn. If he was the one who had taken Finn, had she just provoked him further? With every footstep, regret for such an impulsive move dug itself deeper under her skin. It was beginning to dawn on her that she might not see Finn bounding around the corner – not ever. And the thought of him alone and injured or afraid was like being dragged under by a giant wave. The sky was turning orange and gray as the sun descended and the streetlights in town began to glow in anticipation of nightfall. She got to the house where the *Chronicle* had its offices and tried the door. It was locked.

"No!" screamed Jude. She grabbed the knob and rattled the door. "Jack? I have the money. Please open up!"

There was no sound from within. She pounded on the door, begging for it to open. But after a while, when it was clear that Jack's father had shut the offices knowing full well that she was returning with cash, when it was clear that Bragg Falls had won again, Jude slumped against the door and let out a wail.

A few blocks away, a dog chained in someone's backyard answered with his own lonely howl.

CHAPTER 21

The gathering dusk hadn't dampened Bragg Falls' school spirit. Nor had the fact that the home team was down by seventeen points to start the second half. The band hammered out snatches of a recent pop song while a flock of brightly-costumed cheerleaders fluttered their pom-poms as they danced in the glare of the stadium lights.

Caroline sat on one of the lower metal bleachers with her hoodie pulled sullenly over her head, hands tucked under her armpits. Sophie had settled herself a few feet away and was checking the wrapper on a granola bar for the number of calories.

"Why can't we tell her?" Caroline tried again. Although they'd had the same conversation a few minutes ago, she hoped the snack she'd proffered might put her friend in a better mood.

"It's a private matter, I told you." Sophie unwrapped the granola bar and ate a third of it in one bite.

Caroline threw up her hands in frustration. "What is your problem, Soph? She'd know what to do."

"No," Sophie insisted as forcefully as was possible with her mouth full.

"Why not? Come on, your dad would want us to."

"No, he would most definitely not, so just drop it! I don't want to talk about my dad," cried Sophie, her voice becoming shrill. "And by the way, Jude Brannock doesn't walk on water."

"I don't think that," Caroline said darkly.

"Yeah, you do. It's obvious," said Sophie, going on the attack. "Everything is Jude this and Jude that. You meet her in the park, she comes over to your house for dinner, she's *soooo* intense! Why don't you go live with her?"

"Don't be ridiculous," said Caroline.

Jealousy and anger hummed in the space between them as they watched the game in silence. Minutes later, two varsity cheerleaders strolled by. No doubt, thought Caroline, using their break to go fix their hair and makeup. One of them whispered to her friend and shot an undisguised smirk in Caroline's direction.

"Yo, Nancy. You got somethin' on your mind other than failing U.S. History?" Caroline threw out. She had to take it out on somebody.

Nancy stopped and leaned insolently into her hip, flipping a lock of blond hair over her shoulder. "Well, now that you ask," she said, "I was just telling Raylene that my aunt is a hair stylist in town. She could, you know, fix your hair if you wanted."

Caroline glowered at her. "I like it the way it is."

"Suit yourself," said Nancy, rolling her eyes. "I'm just trying to help."

"No help to me if I end up looking like you," Caroline retorted. To show her cool contempt, she reached into her pocket and pulled out a crushed pack of Marlboros that she was holding for Jack. She lit one up and pretended to inhale.

Nancy's comrade weighed in, "Ooo, you can get so busted for smoking on school property, you know."

"Well, it wouldn't be the first time," Nancy happily reminded Raylene. "Caroline's yearbook caption will be 'voted most likely to fuck up.'"

Caroline blew smoke in her direction. "Yeah, and just like Paul Revere I'd ride ahead of you warning everyone, 'the bitches are coming, the bitches are coming!'"

"You are so pathetic, Chapel," said Nancy disgustedly.

"She's not retarded like *you*," said Sophie, finding her voice.

Affronted that the girl with the lowest status had dared to butt in, Raylene turned to her and snapped, "Why don't you lose thirty pounds, then you can open your sorry, fat mouth."

Sophie paled and looked to Caroline to shoot back a stinging remark. They were a pack – even if a small one – being attacked by the alpha girls. But Caroline wasn't up to the task; she sat wordless, puffing away at her cigarette and allowing Raylene's cut at Sophie to take full effect. Sophie waited for one more hopeful moment before grabbing her backpack and stumbling off like wounded prey. It wasn't until Caroline saw the exchange of a victory glance between the alpha girls that she came alive. She tossed her lit cigarette at their feet. "Get out of here," she warned, "before I knock you both on your ass."

As they pranced off, Caroline shrunk into herself, knowing she had spoken too little, too late; loyalty was crucial against the dark forces in high school. But Caroline was still seething over her friend's stubbornness. She looked around to track down a potential ride home and noticed a man sit down on the bench a few feet away. He was wearing a windbreaker and khakis, and with a pair of black framed glasses looked like any other parent, except a lot cooler, thought Caroline. His dark blond hair was cut stylishly long and he reminded her of an English movie star whose name slipped her mind.

He gave her an understated smile and asked casually, "How come Bragg Falls runs up the middle every single time? It looks like they've got a decent quarterback, why doesn't he throw any passes?"

Programmed to be cautious around strangers, Caroline mumbled, "Apparently it's the only play they know."

"Ah," he exclaimed, as if that was a satisfactory answer.

"They have a lousy coach, or so my dad says."

"Your dad probably knows his football then."

"Sometimes I wonder if that's all he knows," said Caroline.

The man laughed. "Aw, I'm a dad, too. Don't be too hard on us. My name's Dave, by the way. I coach up at the state university."

He leaned over and held out his hand which was warm and strong, and when he flashed an infectious grin, Caroline blushed. "What do you coach?" she asked.

"Ladies' track."

She sat up a bit straighter. "I run track, well ... I used to."

"No kidding." He sized her up. "Yeah, you look like a runner. What's your name?"

"Caroline. Chapel."

On the field below, it was third and eight, and the Bragg Falls offensive line ran a play up the middle for a gain of two yards. Dave stole a sideways glance at Caroline and made a point of trying to keep a straight face. Confederates now, she put a hand over her mouth to cover the smile that itched to break free.

"Excuse me, gotta call my wife," said Dave, pulling out his cell phone. "Ah, shoot. No battery. And I promised I'd call her." He looked to either side in case an answer to his problem lay within reach and then had an idea. "Say, Caroline, do you have a cell phone I could borrow just for a minute?"

"Sure." She retrieved her phone from her hoodie pocket and handed it to him.

He started to dial a number and then stopped. "I can't hear myself think with all this noise. Would it be okay if I made the call over where it's a little quieter? Maybe you would keep your eye on my bag. I'll be right back." He slid a leather attaché case toward her feet, then got up and walked out of sight behind the bleachers.

Caroline wasn't too concerned. If he was going to steal her cell phone, he wouldn't have left his briefcase with her, and even she could tell from its buttery-soft texture and gleaming brass clasps that it was expensive. Plus, he was a coach at the state university. In any event, he returned before she had too much time to ponder.

"Thanks. You're a life-saver," he said, handing back her phone. "Well, I told my wife I'd be home by dinner, so I better hustle." He picked up his bag and gave Caroline a friendly wink. "Maybe I'll see you on the track team."

The teenager was too young to spot deception, but old enough to be charmed, and when he left, she felt the weight of depression descend. To be on a well-coached college track team was like a dream, but she remembered that college wasn't in her future. Fate had other plans ... too bad, she'd never get to ask him how he lost part of his finger.

* * *

The stillness in the sanctuary enveloped Jude in a cloud of apprehension. She hadn't been inside a church for a long time, unable to reconcile a Christian god's call for compassion with the terrible things she'd seen some of these same Christians do to animals. The sign outside said it was a Methodist Church, and although Jude knew almost nothing about its doctrine, still she felt drawn to it in case some elusive deity might reside in an empty church and secretly care about lost animals.

Keeping her eyes on the giant gold cross behind the altar, Jude's footsteps echoed on the flagstone floor and her fingers brushed against the ends of the wooden pews as she made her way down the center aisle. The doors had been left unlocked and the wall sconces were lit, so she supposed anyone could just walk right in. She slipped into one of the pews about halfway down the aisle. Before one prayed, did one have to atone for not coming to church? Would a simple apology do? From attending Mass in her early childhood, she remembered the words of several prayers, but felt like a hypocrite invoking them now. So she bowed her head and prayed the truth. *God, I don't know who you are or even if I believe in you, but if you're there, please protect Finn. Maybe you won't let him be with me again. I mean, I hope so, I pray so. But if not, just please don't let him be in pain. Please don't let him be in a cage or anything like that, he'll be so scared. I ... I really have nothing to offer you in return, but I'll try to be a better person. Just don't let him suffer.* She tried to think of what else to say but couldn't, so she ended with, *Okay, thanks.*

Footsteps from the back of the church interrupted the silence. Jude swung around, fearful that the man with the camouflage cap had come after her. But in the dim light she saw the figure of a small woman kneeling in the last row. Jude got up and tried to tiptoe up the aisle, so as not to disturb her. But the woman lifted her head as Jude brushed past her pew. It was Alice Chapel.

"Oh, it's you," she exclaimed, and then stammered, "I'm so sorry about ... the other night. My husband was very rude." She could hardly make eye contact.

"Please, no, I totally understand," said Jude, feeling equally awkward. She had shared a beer with this woman's husband just the night before. Nothing happened, but Jude could hardly deny the intimacy of their conversation.

"Emmet has not been himself since his friend Frank died, and he's having a lot of trouble with Caroline," Alice confided. "But that's no excuse. He behaved badly, and that's not who he is at all."

"Mrs. Chapel, really, I–"

"Please call me Alice."

"Okay, no apologies, please. I'm an animal activist. I get thrown out of a lot of places. Oh dear, that didn't come out right." As Jude tried to recover, she saw in Alice's brief smile a glimpse of the young woman Emmet had fallen in love with and it made her feel as though she'd trespassed on their lives. "Well, I don't want to intrude on your private time."

"There's nothing private in the eyes of God," said Alice. "I actually came in to say a little prayer for Caroline. I think she needs more help than we can give her right now." She looked searchingly into Jude's eyes. "Do you mind my asking..." Jude was afraid Alice would make too much of her presence in church and request that they pray together, but she finished, "What are you doing here in Bragg Falls?"

Regardless of her beliefs, it seemed wrong to be dishonest in this place, so Jude told her that she was supposed to meet with Frank who had wanted to share certain information about animal treatment at D&M.

Alice looked away at the mention of the animals, unwilling to meet Jude's eyes. "Is that what Emmet meant when he mentioned a video?" she asked.

"Frank documented some of the things that are going on with a hidden camera, yes."

"Has ... anyone found the video?"

"Not that I know of."

Alice swallowed hard. "What do you think happened to it?"

"I really couldn't say."

Another question seemed to play on Alice's lips, but after a moment, she dropped her head and mumbled, "Poor Frank. And poor Verna. I honestly don't know what she'll do without him."

"They were very close?" asked Jude sympathetically.

"Goodness, yes. More than any couple I know."

CHAPTER 22

Jude rapped again on Verna's door, louder this time. There *had* been movement inside the house, she was sure of it. "Verna, it's me, Jude Brannock. Please open the door."

A cold, light rain had begun to fall, beading up on the metal railing of the front steps and plastering leaves against the sidewalk. Jude blew on her ungloved hands, then balled her hand into a fist and pounded on the door. "Verna! Come on. I know you're in there. I have to talk to you – it's important."

Next door a curtain moved aside, revealing a disapproving, wary face. When Jude responded with a forced smile, the curtain dropped back. Finally, Jude heard the chain on the lock and let her shoulders drop, only to realize that Verna had put the chain *on* to keep the door from opening more than a few inches.

"Go away," said Verna gruffly.

Matching her brusqueness, Jude said, "You lied to me, Verna. You told me you didn't know anything about Frank's video. But I keep running into people who tell me how *close* you and Frank were, how deep your relationship was, and it got me thinking. That's why you never seemed too upset about Frank keeping it a secret from you ... because it wasn't a secret, was it? You knew all along."

The widow stared through the door opening like an animal trapped in a cage.

But Jude felt the same way and wouldn't back down. "Look, somebody took my dog, and maybe they've killed him," she said. "If it has something to do with the video, I deserve to know, and I'm not leaving until I find out. Why did you lie to me?"

"I didn't know who you were," Verna replied bitterly. "Frank told me he'd contacted someone at your organization. But he got the number from a website, for goodness sake. How was I supposed to know?"

"Who did you think I was?" demanded Jude.

"I thought maybe ... from Marshfield."

"And now?"

Verna conceded, "I believe you."

"Would you let me in then?"

"I can't."

Jude leaned her forehead against the door frame trying to tamp down the frustration building inside. "At least tell me what happened."

When Verna next spoke, she sounded less obliging than bone-deep weary. "I knew what Frank was doing. I'm the one who suggested it. No one was responding to his letters or his phone calls. He lost *hope* – the only thing he had that kept him going. No one would listen. His drinking got worse, he was angry all the time. One night we had an argument and he hit me. I told him, 'Next time it'll be Sophie, so you'd better find a way through this to save your soul.' He decided to take them on himself, so he got one of those little spy cameras and started taping. I saw some of it – men beating the pigs with iron pipes, kicking them, putting their cigarettes out on the poor animals' faces, and all the brutality of getting the hogs up on the chain, some of 'em still alive and struggling."

Jude knew there was more and tried to draw Verna out, saying, "You know as well as I do, that kind of abuse goes on all the time, and not just at Marshfield. Frank captured something else. He said it was something explosive."

"Yes, it was some conversation between Bob Warshauer and someone from the corporation. It made him furious and he was sure that it would really hurt Marshfield. He was going to play it for me but he never got the chance because Bob found out. He came to Frank and told him he was going to have to give it up – the camera and all the footage. He threatened him, threatened us."

Jude broke in, incredulous, "He physically threatened you?"

"Not in so many words. But Frank got scared."

"Why didn't he go to the police?"

"And say *what*?" demanded Verna. "I've been secretly taping the operations of D&M – the industry that employs half this town – and now they've found out and are demanding I turn the tape over so I can't give it to an animal welfare organization?"

"So they knew about me?"

"I think they did, but I don't know how. Frank was supposed to meet someone that the company had sent from Raleigh last Friday night after work. We knew he was going to get fired, but he was going to try to get some severance out of them. Afterwards, he was supposed to call me and let me know what happened, but he never did. And I couldn't reach him. I figured his phone died again."

Jude wished that Verna would open the door and let her in, but as wet and cold as she was, she didn't press it as long as Verna was talking. "The parts of the video that Frank showed you ... how did you see it?"

"On his computer. He'd download each day's footage on his laptop."

"The same computer Sheriff Ward brought to you the day I was here?"

"Yes, but I looked and the video is gone. It's like it was wiped off."

Jude leaned in close to the crack in the door. "But the pain killer prescription and the research about fatal doses of oxycodone – that *was* on the computer. Do you think that really was Frank's doing?"

"I don't know," Verna grieved. "He felt like such a failure when he got caught, like he'd let everybody down, and almost worse than losing his job, he was afraid he'd lose all his friends. At first I thought maybe it was too much for him. But he was a fighter, and in my heart of hearts I don't believe he would leave me and Sophie like that."

"If they weren't Frank's computer entries, who put them there?"

Verna's answer came out haltingly, "Marshfield. Someone. I don't think Bob Warshauer is smart enough to do something like that, but it's a big company."

"Could the Sheriff's office be involved? Could they have erased the tape from Frank's computer?"

"You'd have to ask them."

As if Jude herself had summoned the patrol car with her question, a blue oscillating light swirled out of the darkness behind her. She looked over her shoulder to see one of the County Sheriff's cars pulling up behind hers.

"I'm sorry," said Verna. "I had to call them. I ... I made a deal with Bob and I'm not supposed to talk to you."

"A deal? He offered you money?"

Two deputies exited the patrol car, mirror images as they adjusted their trooper style hats.

"Don't you get high and mighty with me," hissed Verna angrily. "We don't have Frank's income, the life insurance won't pay ... what do you expect me to do? I have a child to think about."

Jude remembered her last visit to Verna and the mess in the house. She had precious little time. "Did Frank make a copy of the video? Is that what you were looking for the other day?"

Verna looked beyond her at one of the deputies who was peering into the back of the Subaru, his hand lightly resting on his service weapon. The other deputy started toward Jude.

"Did you find it?" breathed Jude.

"Jude Brannock?" asked the deputy as he came up the steps. He knew very well who she was. "Brannock?" he repeated more forcefully. "You're under arrest for harassment. Come with me."

"Just one second, please," Jude begged.

But he had already gotten out the handcuffs.

Verna's frightened eyes appeared through the slit in the door and Jude caught a glimpse of her shaking her head. No, she hadn't found a copy. Jude persisted, "Could Frank have given it to somebody? His friend Howard Bisbee? Emmet Chapel?"

"Put your hands behind your back."

She closed the front door, but Verna's voice came through loud and clear, "I don't know anything about that. I can't help you." Whether it was directed at her or for the deputy's benefit, Jude didn't know. She put her hands behind her as he slipped a plastic cuff around her wrists and tightened it. "Let's go," he commanded.

The deputy took Jude by the elbow and steadied her when she tripped on the second step, "Watch out," he warned, "it's slippery."

Yes, it is, she thought. Ever since she arrived in Bragg Falls – slippery and perilous.

CHAPTER 23

Sheriff Ward's keys jangled while he searched for the right one to open the cell door. Jude remained seated inside on a cot bolted to the wall, trying not to appear too eager. She couldn't be sure, but from the exasperated look on the Sheriff's face, he had probably been on the phone with Elizabeth Crowley, the attorney for The Kinship. Elizabeth – no one called her Liz – had that effect on a lot of people. As if by magic, she could pull legal arguments out of thin air, making opposing counsel flip through statutes in a fruitless effort to make his or her vanishing case reappear. Even when her motions and briefs were on shaky legal ground, she often got what she wanted simply by showing up. The long legs and flawless skin were combined with an elegance and grace that were downright intimidating ... a vegan goddess.

"You're free to go," said Ward tersely. But he dragged his feet opening the cell door.

"You spoke with our attorney?" Jude asked.

"I did. I could have kept you overnight, but at this point, I don't know which one of you I'd less want to deal with."

Almost sympathetically, Jude said, "Elizabeth's tough."

"I'm sure it's a necessity since you animal rights people must end up on the wrong side of the law pretty often," said Ward. "But she's not the reason you're getting out. Verna Marino has decided not to press charges." He opened the cell door and stood aside to let Jude pass.

But she didn't move. "Can I talk to you?" she asked.

"You gotta be kidding."

Hearing from Verna that the video had been erased from Frank's computer raised questions about Ward's connection with Marshfield and what, if any, involvement he had in Frank's death. But a part of her believed that Ward was on the level and since she was already in deep, Jude decided to swim out even farther. "I'm not convinced that Frank Marino committed suicide," she stated flatly.

The implied accusation hung in the air like a stink bomb and Ward moved into the cell as if he could block it from passing through the bars. He leaned against the wall opposite the cot and crossed his arms. "This better be good," he said, his teeth clenched.

"I told you about the videotape that Frank made at the plant. Well, I think he got something else on the tape besides the systematic animal abuse that's going on inside."

Ward just stared at her.

"You have to understand, part of what we do is getting footage of this kind of institutionalized cruelty, and there's plenty of people who don't want to see that come to light. Folks around here have made that very clear to me. But Frank discovered something potentially more damaging to Marshfield, something that went beyond the industry's systemic abuse. He as much as told me so. And Marshfield was aware of it. They found out what he had – I don't know how – and tried to coerce him into giving up the video, his camera, everything."

"Did he give it to them? Whoever *them* is..."

"I think he probably did."

"So if he gave them what they wanted, why murder him?" Ward cracked his knuckles, decidedly unimpressed with her theory.

"They couldn't be sure there wasn't a copy made. And if there was, only Frank could authenticate it. The video loses value in court without testimony about how, when and where it was made–"

"I've been in court, Brannock, I know what *authenticate* means. You may think that because you're from the big city that we're hicks down here."

"You didn't let me finish," insisted Jude. "Without Frank, the video could well have had evidentiary problems at a trial, but it doesn't mean it would fall flat in the court of public opinion. In a few days, the state legislature is going to pass a bill that makes it a felony to record or distribute photographic evidence of animal abuse at places like D&M. All well and good for Marshfield long term, but as soon as that bill goes to the Governor for his signature, the media's ears will be up, and if they're not, my organization and some others will make sure they are. We hand over footage of the kind Frank made, a lot of people are going to look real bad. Marshfield can protest that it was fabricated all they want, but the proverbial shit will have hit the fan."

"So what are you saying?"

"I'm saying that Marshfield cannot let anyone get their hands on a copy of Frank's video – particularly me."

Ward pushed himself away from the wall and for a second, Jude worried he might strike her. But he simply leaned into her, the muscles in his jaw twitching as he ground his teeth. "And what makes you think there is a copy of this alleged videotape floating around?"

She'd couldn't discern if his demand was arising from a police officer's natural desire to get to the bottom of things or from a corrupt need to find out what she knew so he could take it back to Marshfield. Either way, there was an intensity in his eyes that stopped Jude cold and she felt her confidence wane. "I surmise that there is ... uh, someone searching my hotel room," she stammered. "... the threats to me, my dog..."

His eyes burned into her as he said, "We did a thorough investigation that will hold up in any court of law. Frank Marino committed suicide and you've said nothing to make me think differently. You and your whole organization – you make a living at conspiracy theories. You got something solid, give it to me. Otherwise, I don't want to see you again."

With that, he strode angrily down the hallway, leaving such a trail of hostility that she hesitated to follow. But after a moment, she figured she'd better take advantage of the open cell door and get out before he changed his mind.

*   *   *

The Sheriff's final words should have hastened her departure from Bragg Falls, but she wasn't leaving without Finn. Jude went back to the motor inn, parking her car around the side where it couldn't be seen from the road. After double checking the chain on the door, she called in.

"Elizabeth sprung you from the slammer, eh?" asked CJ. "Any news on Finn? Gordon says he'll send someone down if you need. Finn's our hero, you know."

"Thanks, but I'm not sure that *more* activists in Bragg Falls are going to help."

"Whatever you need. Listen, I learned something. I did a check on that company PharmaRX where Frank allegedly bought the pain killers. It's legit, well legal anyway, a Mexican drug dispensary. Anyone can go on line, fill out a form and they'll have one of their so-called *doctors* authorize a prescription. I verified Frank's purchase, but here's the thing ... there's no confirmation that the order was actually filled and shipped. I did a little scam on the shipping department and they had no record of anything going out to Frank Marino."

"What does that mean?"

"It's not conclusive, especially since most of the people operating the company don't speak English. But it could be that the oxycodone that killed Frank didn't come from PharmaRX and that someone down there got paid off to enter a phony prescription request into their computer. That entry might be enough to throw the cops off if they decided to look into it. Speaking of computers, did you ever get a chance to look at Frank's?"

"No, but I found out from Verna that she saw parts of the video on his computer shortly before Frank died. When the Sheriff returned the computer that the cops found in the car, the file was gone."

"Somewhere in there it got erased," concluded CJ.

"I guess. So..."

"Frank could have erased it ... or someone in the Sheriff's office. You did tell me that he showed up awfully fast when you were taking photos of the plant. How did he know you were there? Could be D&M is cozy with the local Sheriff."

Jude recalled how defensive Ward had been when she hinted at foul play in Frank's death. "It wouldn't be the first time," she said somberly.

"Let me add one more thing," broached CJ. "It's possible to use a restore option to backdate new input."

"Give it to me in English."

"Okay. The order to PharmaRX purportedly sent from Frank's computer? The searches that Frank did on oxycodone? I'm speculating, but if someone who knew what they were doing got their hands on his laptop, they could make it look like he placed the order and did the searches *before* he died, when in fact the information was input at a later date."

"You mean input *after* he died. How could they do that?"

"Well, you set the specified program back to an earlier date ... you really want me to explain how to do it?"

"Not really. But I do want to understand what you're implying ... that someone might have doctored Frank's computer to make it look like he was contemplating suicide?"

With that troubling question still hanging in the air, Jude promised to check in later. She shut off the lights and sat on the bed, trying not to imagine her life without Finn, trying to forget the slow march of helpless creatures driven through an assembly line of pain and fear, trying not to think about the impenetrable wall of power and secrecy behind which the Marshfield corporation operated.

She wasn't aware of having dozed off until she heard rapping on the front door. She sat up on the bed and glanced at the clock. It was almost midnight. The knock came again and she swung her feet over the side and tiptoed to the window. Through a slit in the curtain she saw a man at her door. She recognized the slope of his shoulders and drew back, her mind racing.

"Jude, it's Emmet Chapel," he said softly.

Could he possibly know something about Finn? She opened the door as far as the chain would allow. Emmet stood framed in the doorway, hands dug deep in his jeans pockets.

"Is this about Finn?" she asked.

"Who?"

"My dog."

"No ... no. Can I come in?"

"No," replied Jude. But her voice, even on the single syllable, wavered. The investigator in her was now wide awake.

"Five minutes. Please, I just need to talk to you."

Jude slid the chain off its track and opened the door. He walked slowly to the bed and sat on the edge as she turned on the overhead light. The stark glare magnified the lines in his face and the gray at his temples. He held up his hand to shield himself from the unforgiving light and Jude switched it off, leaving them barely illuminated by the glow of the streetlights straining through the thin curtains. She perched warily on the desk opposite him.

"How did you know where to find me?" she asked.

"Everyone knows you're here."

She barked out a short laugh. "Great. What do you want?" she asked.

When he looked up, she could see the longing in his eyes and her apprehension came flooding back, not because she felt threatened, but because she felt the same longing.

"You shouldn't have come," she said.

He nodded, but made no move to leave. "I needed to see you," he breathed.

Jude put up her guard although he looked as worn to the bone as she felt. "I thought we covered this," she said harshly. "I'm not in the business of human salvation. I barely keep my head above water doing the work I do. Besides, someone stole my dog who I love very much and to be honest, I'm just hanging on right now."

"Do you know who took him?" he asked.

"No."

"I'm sorry," said Emmet. "Maybe I can help."

"Maybe you can. Why don't you start by telling me about Frank Marino."

Confusion creased his brow. "What are you talking about?"

Jude felt reckless, as though she were speeding through a dark tunnel, unwilling to slow down until she saw daylight. "Were you with him the night he died?" she asked.

"Yeah..." Emmet replied uncertainly.

"In the car."

"What car? You mean his car when he took an overdose? Christ, no! I was with him at the Lazy Cat. I never saw him after that." When Jude continued glaring at him, Emmet exclaimed, "What are you implying? That I had something to do with Frank's death? Are you crazy, he was my *friend*." Emmet's injury seemed genuine and it took a moment for him to see where she was going. "You still think Frank was murdered, don't you?" He dropped his head in his hands. "The video ... that goddamn video. Well, it wasn't me," he said, his words muffled.

"It crossed your mind that they killed him, though, didn't it?" asked Jude.

A grieving sigh escaped through his hands and he shook his head. She didn't know if it was because he didn't know anything or because he wouldn't say.

"Are you okay?" asked Jude more gently.

"Could I have some water?"

She went over to the kitchenette, filled a mug with tap water and brought it over. He took it gratefully and drank. "Frank was right, it's very bad there," he finally said.

"At the plant? I know."

"No you don't," he said. A bit of light caught his eyes and in them a look of desperation. "Something happened today."

He didn't speak for a long time, and when he did, his voice sounded hollow. "I had to put Tim Vernon back on the stunner. The new kid couldn't handle the pressure and was slowing everything down. I thought Vernon was going to be okay, I really did. But at the end of the shift, this guy named Crank and another kid drug in a sow from outside. No one knew why she couldn't walk, it didn't look like she was disabled – she just looked used up. I heard Crank yelling, trying to get Vernon over to where the sow was laying to stun her. Vernon was blowing them off, saying he wouldn't leave his area and stun a pregnant pig. And Crank gets in his face and calls him a 'bullshitter,' says he doesn't know what he's talking about, which is the wrong thing to say to Tim Vernon. I didn't really hear what else they said ... it all happened so fast. But before anyone can stop him, Vernon takes his hunting knife and goes over to the hog and slices her belly open. And he's right. There's piglets spilling out onto the floor and they're alive!

"That might have been the end of it, but Vernon points his knife at Crank and says, 'What did I tell ya, asshole?' and starts to walk away like ... nothin' happened. Maybe Crank was juiced, but he jumps Vernon from behind. By the time we get him off, they're both cut bad and it's all a bloody mess."

Jude put her hand over her mouth.

"It's my fault. Vernon's a psycho, but I put him back on the job. He's the only one who can get them through fast enough." Emmet raked the hair back from his face with both hands. "And then fucking Warshauer comes down to the floor and screams at me. You know why? Not because there's a knife fight on the floor, not because some poor pregnant sow with babies in her belly gets cut open while she's still alive – because I shut the goddamn line down. I stopped the chain."

The words poured out of him, breaching a protective wall. "I don't know what to do. I don't know where to go," he broke down. "I don't even know who I am anymore. All I ever wanted was to provide for my family and the harder I try, the more they hate me. Alice is scared. And Caroline is so messed up – there's something wrong with her. My son Will is the only one who still believes in me ... but he won't for long." A single tear oozed from his eye and trailed along the scar on his face.

Jude went over and sat next to him. She touched the tear, feeling it dissolve into her skin, and then unable to help herself, she traced the vivid, white scar gently with her finger.

Emmet caught her hand and held it to his cheek – then to his mouth. He kissed her palm, the inside of her wrist, and began to move his lips along her inner arm with a tenderness and need that aroused something deep inside her. Jude weakened in the wake of his sensuality. God, how she missed being with someone who wanted her. So many nights in sterile hotel rooms, isolated as an investigator or camouflaged as an undercover. When his mouth found hers, she yielded. Their kiss was deep and long. But finally Jude pulled away and their eyes met – it was wrong and they both knew it.

"Please go," she said, sure that if he didn't leave now, it would be too late.

If he had reached out one more time, the night might have taken them both in its arms and rocked them onto a different path. But he didn't. The bed creaked when he stood, the sound nearly covering the soft buzz of his phone. As he headed to the door, he pulled it from his back pocket and stared at the screen.

He closed his eyes. "What is it, Alice?" His back straightened and he swore softly. "I ... I'm at the hospital checking on someone from work. Yeah, I'll be right home."

When he hung up, Jude asked, "Is something wrong?"

"Don't worry, it's not your concern." Emmet walked out of the hotel room without looking back.

*   *   *

It felt like forever, but it was only minutes later that Jude's phone rang. Entirely spent, she had no expectation, no intuition left. She didn't even bother to look at the number on the screen, but answered it dully, "Yes?"

"Is this Jude?" She recognized the voice. "This is Jack Delaney. I think I know where your dog is."

Chapter 24

Emmet walked into the kitchen where Alice paced restlessly, her cell phone clutched in her hand like a life line.

"Where have you been?" she demanded. "Oh, right. The Lazy Cat again."

"Alice, please," he cautioned, closing his eyes to the overwhelming sense of isolation that enveloped him. Nothing new. Sometimes just walking through the front door was enough to trigger it. At home he had to be strong, he had to lock up what he did all day into a secret compartment where it festered and ate him alive from the inside. He couldn't talk about it with his wife; she was stressed and anxious enough as it was. God knows, he couldn't tell his children. He couldn't talk about it with the guys at work – they were as ready as he was to leave the slaughterhouse behind each day. Clock out, then purge the smell of blood and fear with a hot shower and a six-pack.

It was funny, he thought, Jude Brannock was in all respects the enemy, and yet with her he didn't feel quite so alone. She hated what he did – but she understood him. And that created a craving he had never quite felt before.

"Are you listening to me, Emmet?" asked Alice.

"Yes, yes. Caroline's probably with that kid Jack," he said, taking a plastic cup from the dish drainer and filling it with tap water.

"I told her that if she ever went off with him again without telling me, there would be severe consequences," Alice said without conviction.

Emmet drained the water and smacked his cup down on the counter with a distinctive crack. "Well, she doesn't listen to you, Alice," he said harshly. "She doesn't listen to me. She's a selfish little shit who doesn't give a good goddamn about anybody but herself."

"Please don't be angry." Alice collapsed on a kitchen chair. "Please, not tonight. I just want to find her."

"She'll turn up," said Emmet.

"How can you be so sure?"

"Because she's done this before," he argued.

"Maybe if you didn't always see the worst in her, she wouldn't feel the need to run away," responded Alice angrily. Tears that she had held back for hours began to slide down her cheeks. "I'm just so afraid that with all her talk about the end of the world and death and destruction, what if this time she's gone off to ... to make it happen?"

The thought that his wife could be right flooded Emmet with worry, but he slipped back into his role of steadfast husband and father, and he placed a comforting hand on her shoulder. "Don't worry, she's just acting out. But I'll go look for her. Did you talk to Verna? Maybe Sophie knows where she is."

"No, she doesn't," replied Alice. "I've called Verna twice already. Caroline went over there after dinner, but Verna says that the girls had some kind of fight and Caroline left."

"You tried to call her, I guess."

"I've left so many messages. I don't know, maybe she isn't getting them. Verna thought that she might have gone looking for Jude Brannock. I think Caroline has some kind of hero worship for her, so maybe Verna's right. Supposedly she's staying at the Motor Inn." Alice suddenly stopped herself. "Oh, I can't believe I didn't think of that. I'll call them." From one of the kitchen drawers she dug out a dog-eared yellow pages. "What is it called ... a motel, a hotel?"

"She's not there," said Emmet.

"Verna thought she was," said Alice, paging through the directory. "*Caroline* isn't at the motel."

"I'll bet that's exactly where she went."

Unable to stave off the coming storm, Emmet said, "Trust me, Caroline isn't with Jude."

At his casual use of Jude's first name, Alice raised her head from the directory, confusion furrowing her brow. "How ... how could you know that?"

The answer seemed to drop from his mouth of its own accord. "I was just there." He tried to avert his eyes, but the look of bewilderment then understanding and finally of betrayal in his wife's face held him prisoner.

"I see," said Alice, her voice barely audible. She let the directory slip from her fingers and went into the bedroom, closing the door quietly but with a finality that told him the hurt was too deep for any explanation ... and he had none to offer.

*   *   *

A front had pushed the clouds eastward and cleared the skies, leaving a sickle blade of a moon slicing into the black night. Jude drew in next to the truck parked behind the gas station. No one got out of the truck at her arrival, but it did match the description Jack had given her – "a brown piece of shit with the rear bumper holding on by a thread." In fact, the bumper looked relatively secure, tied to the undercarriage with baling wire and duct tape.

The cab's passenger door opened and a hand reached out and beckoned. Jude slipped into the front seat and found herself next to Caroline. Jack was at the wheel, his ink-stained fingers balancing a can of Miller Lite.

Jude eyed Caroline cautiously. "Your folks know where you are?"

This elicited only a shrug and Jude let it go, unwilling to play social worker for the moment. She was more concerned with what Jack knew about Finn. "Where is he?"

"We're going to take you," he said.

"Why don't you just tell me," Jude urged.

Caroline interjected, "You'd never find it on your own, and you can't just waltz in there. Jack knows a back way."

"Is he all right?"

"Wish I could tell you," said Jack. "I don't know for sure he's even there. But I heard some things."

"Maybe we should call the police," suggested Jude. "Let them handle this."

The two teens shared a look. "I wouldn't advise that," said Jack. "Besides, I really don't want my name involved, nor do I want anyone with a badge even close to my truck."

It was then that Jude noticed the unmistakable aroma of marijuana that permeated the cab. "Christ, have you been smoking dope?" she asked, wondering how reliable Jack was.

"No," Caroline insisted.

"It sure smells like it," said Jude.

Jack waved her concern away. "It's old. So, you want us to help you or not? You can follow in your car, but once we get to where we're going, you have to do it my way. You don't know who you're dealing with."

Jude stayed close enough to Jack's truck to smell the exhaust as he wound through the rural roads leading away from town. Soon, he turned off and she bounced along after him on a rutted dirt road until it came to a sudden end. There were no houses anywhere in sight. Jack got out and stood peering through a thicket of pines.

As Jude walked up to join him, he asked, "Do you have a flashlight?"

"In the car." When she retrieved one that she kept for emergencies, he advised, "Use as little light as possible, and if you hear anything, turn it off and don't move."

Jude had to wonder where the hell they were going and only hoped that the two teens were overdramatizing the rescue plan. But she also remembered that Jack was a smart kid, and his abundance of caution gave her pause. He led them into the woods where the tall pines had laid down a carpeting of dried needles that deadened their footsteps. The landscape soon gave way to trickier footing with brambles grabbing at their lower legs. At the sound of a dog barking in the distance, Jack put out a hand. They listened for a moment until Jude shook her head; the pitch was too high to be Finn.

Slowly, the trio continued until they were at the edge of a clearing carved into a hill. Lights burned from the first floor of a gray split-level house at the top of the slope. A dirt driveway wound down from the front to a free-standing garage about a hundred yards below. Midway between the house and the garage was what appeared to be a small shed with a row of garbage cans hugging one wall. A young man wearing jeans and no shirt trudged up the steps to a covered porch at the front of the house where a wiry hound was chained. The dog strained against his collar, barking at the intruders only he could smell. The young man slapped his thigh in irritation. "Shut up, Hardy, or I'll leave you out here all night." The dog paid no attention.

A heavyset man carrying a 12-guage shotgun emerged to stand framed in the doorway. "What the hell is he making so much noise fer?" he groused.

"Beats me, Pop. He's caught the smell of somethin' out there."

"Coyotes, probably."

"Could be a raccoon sniffing around."

Suddenly, the hound stiffened and the fur on his neck stood up. He trotted to the far side of the porch as far as his tether would go and sniffed the air. When he began to bark again, the larger man unhooked him and dragged him inside by his collar. For good measure he kicked the dog in the haunches, causing him to yelp. "Git in thar," he thundered. Then Roy Mears came back out and stood next to his son, looking out over their property.

"I don't know, that's not his coyote bark," said the young man cautiously.

"Who cares what it is. Keep yer freakin' dog quiet 'cause I'm going back to bed. Don't think I won't shoot him along with the coyotes."

They went inside and closed the door; the lights went out. Jude released the breath she had been holding and met Jack's eyes. Now she understood his precautions, guessing that she wasn't the only one who had gotten on the wrong side of Roy Mears. At this moment it didn't matter if Mears was a dog thief – they were on the private property of a man who would undoubtedly shoot first and ask questions later. And in this stand-your-ground state, he was within his rights to do so. "How did you hear that he took Finn?" she whispered to Jack.

"Just around," replied Jack. "Somebody said Mears was bragging to folks about getting himself a new hunting dog that looked like a Rottweiler, so I figured it might be him." He touched her on the arm and murmured, "I'll be right back."

Before she could stop him, he had slunk off through the ferns and crabgrass at the edge of the clearing. Jude now regretted allowing the two teenagers to get involved; confirming her misgivings, she became aware of Caroline trembling next to her.

"Are you okay?" asked Jude softly.

"No," replied the girl in a small, quavering voice. "I'm afraid for Finn. Why did they take him? Was it because of the video Frank made?"

Jude turned her head sharply. "What do you know about that?" she whispered harshly.

Pulling her hoodie down over her head as if she could block out what she was thinking and feeling, Caroline began to sob. She could barely get the words out. "I have it."

"You what?"

"I have the video."

Caroline, the house, the night sky all faded into one crazy blur for a moment. Nothing was making sense. What was she doing with Frank's video? Had he given it to her? Why had she waited until now to say something? There was a rustle in the undergrowth and Jack dropped to his haunches next to them. "The garage is locked," he said breathlessly, "but I'll go around–"

"No," whispered Jude firmly. "Absolutely not. You guys are done, this is my show from here on out."

"You might need help," protested Jack. "What if Finn is in the house?"

"I don't think Mears would do that," said Jude. "He's already got a dog and they might not get along. He wouldn't risk a fight. Both of you go back now."

Jack began to protest, but Jude grabbed his arm. "No," she said into his ear. "Caroline's shaken up, you've got to get her out of here."

She seemed to have prevailed upon his protective nature, because after looking at Caroline's tearstained face, he agreed. He took her by the hand and they disappeared into the darkness.

Jude took a deep breath then crept along the edge of the tree line toward the garage. A familiar adrenaline began to shoot through her system. In her late teens, she'd joined an animal activist group that had put her through a training course designed for midnight entries into testing labs and fur farms. She didn't have the night goggles or tool belt with her now, but she remembered how to stick to the shadows and how to rely on her ears and nose ... most important, she remembered to clear her mind of expected outcomes, keeping it open for any and all possibilities.

She dashed across the grass to the garage. Jack was right, the doors were padlocked. Jude put her head against the wood and made a low whistle that Finn would recognize. What came back was the most beautiful sound she ever heard – his soft, familiar whine. But it didn't come from the garage. It came from the shed.

Forgetting for a moment the danger they'd both be in if Mears heard, Jude sprinted to the shed. It, too, was padlocked. The doors rattled as Finn jumped up from the other side, his nails scrabbling on the wood trying to get to her. "Easy, Finn-boy, easy now," cooed Jude.

The house remained quiet and Jude moved around the perimeter, looking for some way to get him out. On one side was a paned window that faced the house. It was maybe thirty inches square.

She peered through the glass, brushing away cobwebs, heavy with dead insects, but couldn't make out anything but Finn's dark shape. The ledge was level to her chest and she doubted that even if she were able to break the window without rousing Mears that Finn could jump through, not without a running start and not without getting cut by broken glass. Jude crept around the back, running her hands along the wood to feel for loose or rotting boards; maybe she could kick out an opening. As she rounded the next corner, she didn't see the galvanized garbage cans tucked against the side and her foot kicked one of them, loosening the lid and sending it into the other cans.

She froze and waited to see if anyone responded to the sound. Sure enough, a light on the second floor blinked on. Knowing she might have only a minute or two, Jude made a quick decision. She reached down for the garbage can lid to use as a battering ram to break the window. The first time, she made light contact, hoping the noise would scare Finn into the farther reaches of the shed, away from splintering glass. Then angling the edge like a Frisbee, she struck the window as hard as she could. On that blow, the glass shattered and sent shards flying. It sounded like an explosion in her ears. She swung the lid again. More glass broke, but the window casing and crossbars remained intact.

Inside the house, the hound began to bark furiously and all the lights went on. With renewed effort, Jude hit the window again. A piece of glass flew out and punctured the webbing of her hand. She cried out in pain and dropped the lid, while poor Finn mewled in terror inside the shed.

A flood light flared on the front lawn and Roy Mears appeared in the doorway, his shotgun ready. Jude reached down to pick up her battering ram. But her fingers were slick with blood, making it hard to grasp the only weapon she had. Panic set in when she realized she was running out of time and in the rush of fear, she fumbled the lid again.

Suddenly, Jack was beside her. He whipped off his t-shirt, wrapped it around his fist, and started punching at the remaining pieces of the window frame. Caroline appeared with a rock in her hand and the two of them knocked out chunks of wood and glass with each blow.

Then without warning, Mears fired. Two shotgun blasts, one right after the other. The sound was deafening and echoed off the hill. Jack grabbed Jude by the arm to pull her down to safety. A silver dollar-sized hole appeared near the roof of the shed. Jude didn't want to think about how big the exit hole was. But when she looked up, she saw that Jack had knocked out the last of the window.

Jude waved at the two teenagers, "Run! Now!" she yelled. Then she thrust her head into the window opening, finally seeing the light reflected in Finn's eyes. Terrified, he had backed himself into a corner. He'd been imprisoned in this dark, tiny space and now thought he was being attacked. "Come on, Finn, it's okay, it's okay," she coaxed breathlessly. He crouched lower, trembling. He didn't understand.

"Come on, Finn," Jude pleaded.

Jack tugged at her sleeve and shouted, "He's coming!"

"You go. I can't leave Finn!"

Mears had stepped down from the porch and was marching in their direction, inserting more slugs into the shotgun chamber.

Jude screamed at Jack and Caroline, "Go! Go!"

They ran.

Mears took two more steps, then raised his rifle and pointed it directly at her, barely forty yards away – kill range.

A shot rang out and Jude cringed, fully expecting this time to feel the blast. When she realized she had not been hit, she lifted her head. Mears wore a stunned expression and was staring at a spot just inches from his boots. Another shot ricocheted in the dirt, digging a crater even closer to his feet. He jumped back. Someone was shooting at Roy Mears and the shots were coming from the trees behind the house. He cursed and wheeled around to fire back.

In the erupting chaos, Jude turned back to the shed. And at that moment, as if he knew it was his last chance, with a courageous howl, Finn leapt up onto the window ledge and out to freedom.

Mears had forgotten about them. His face a mask of anger and confusion, he fired blindly into the trees. Jude ran for all she was worth with Finn at her heels.

CHAPTER 25

Richard Hillman pressed the phone to his ear to make sure he heard every word.

"I don't think he knew *who* was out there," Bloom was saying. "But he was for damn sure going to shoot somebody, and we need the Chapel girl alive."

"Think he'll call the sheriff's office?"

"Not if he doesn't want to explain why his property is all shot up."

Hillman tightened the sash on his bathrobe and walked over to the bar in his office to grab the decanter of Glenlivet Scotch. If his wife smelled it on his breath when he got back to bed, he'd take some heat for choosing whiskey over a glass of warm milk, but that was the least of his worries. He uncorked the decanter, noticing a slight tremor in his hand. He rationalized that at least he could report to Seldon that Brannock would most likely be on her way. It had been quite unpleasant informing the CEO that someone in Bragg Falls had taken her goddamn dog, because it meant that she wouldn't leave until she got it back. Goddamn rednecks would have screwed everything up. Boy, he just hated to involve Seldon in this kind of detail. Hillman took a large swallow of scotch. "Who is she again?"

"Name's Caroline Chapel. She's the daughter of a new supervisor at the plant. She's been trailing after Brannock for a while now, which is why I got to her phone."

"And what makes you think she has a copy of the tape?" asked Hillman.

"There's texts back and forth from her to Marino's daughter. They're arguing about 'the video' and the Chapel girl taking it. Marino's kid reminds her that it's the only copy and that it's her father's legacy."

Hillman rubbed his red eyes and asked, "Can you find the girl again?"

"Of course."

"Okay, get it."

"What do I do with her?"

"Whatever you have to."

"And Brannock?"

"I repeat. Whatever you have to."

The phone went dead and Hillman poured out another inch of scotch.

*   *   *

"Holy shit!" whooped Jack as they reached the cars. "What happened back there? Who was shooting at Roy Mears?" Out of breath and somewhat giddy, he reached into the glove compartment of his truck to retrieve a small bag of weed. With shaking hands, he rolled a sloppy joint.

"I wish I knew," said Jude, feeling a bit wobbly herself. She kneeled down next to Finn and felt along his back leg. As soon as they had gotten away from Mears and into the woods, she noticed that his limp was much worse. He was able to keep up, but now wouldn't put his back paw to the ground, obviously in pain. Still, he licked her face and pushed his muzzle into her neck while they reconnected, gratefully breathing in each other's warmth and scent.

"Oh my God, you're bleeding," Caroline told Jude.

Jude examined her hand, which had started to throb; the cut was deep and might need stitches. Jack handed her his bandana and she wrapped it around her hand. "Don't worry about me. Let's get Finn into the car. We can't stay here," she said to the teens. "I don't think Mears will come after us, but I'd just as soon not give him that opportunity."

After they helped her lift Finn into the cargo area, she embraced Jack and whispered, "Thank you. Finn thanks you, too." She could feel the heat of a blush against her cheek. "You should go home now. I'm taking Caroline with me. And for Pete's sake," she added, nodding to the joint in his hand, "don't get pulled over."

Back on the main road, neither she nor Caroline spoke for awhile, letting the shock of what had just happened dissipate. Then finally Jude turned to Caroline and said, "You had better tell me everything."

Caroline poured out her confession. It started weeks ago. Sophie had overheard her parents talking about houses in Florida and she knew her father was looking at rentals on his computer. Anxious that they would be separated if the Marinos moved, one night the girls decided to sneak a look. They found Frank's laptop and browsed his files. It wasn't long before they came across the video of D&M. What they saw was disgusting and shocking, yet they couldn't stop watching. Whenever the opportunity arose, they logged in again to see what he had added. It became a kind of ritual, but they never told anyone. It felt secret and dirty, like pornography. One afternoon when Caroline was angry at her dad, she convinced Sophie to make a copy on a DVD. But in the process, they messed up a setting on the computer and her dad found out. Frank was furious. He confronted Sophie and wanted to know if she'd been looking on his computer. When she admitted that she had seen the video, he made her promise she would never look again and would never say anything about it. Sophie felt so guilty she didn't reveal that she had, in fact, made a copy. Two days later her father was dead and she buried the disc in the jumble of her music collection. And then Jude appeared in Bragg Falls. Caroline thought they should give it to her, but Sophie refused – she had given her word and after her dad's death felt an even deeper obligation to keep the video secret. The arguments began.

"Where is it now?" asked Jude.

"Here," said Caroline, digging into her nylon bag. She withdrew an unmarked disc in a clear plastic case and handed it to Jude. Then, as though she had unloaded an unbearable weight, Caroline leaned her head against the back of the seat and pressed her dirty palms against her face. "Sophie's so pissed. She's been sending me mad texts all night. I shouldn't have taken it today, but … I don't know, I had to."

"Why?"

"I wanted to help you … and help the animals."

Jude drove in silence for a minute, unsure what to do. Finally, she said, "I'm taking you home."

"Please no," pleaded Caroline. "I don't want to see my father. I can't look at him now."

Jude guessed the source of her pain. "Your dad's in the video?"

"A couple of times. I knew right away it was him." Caroline's voice was heavy with sorrow, an echo of her father's just hours ago in Jude's hotel room. "What they do in there is horrible. It's so bad what they're doing to the animals. All this time, my dad working there, I never had any idea. There's one part where this man is kicking a pig, trying to make it get up. You can see it's trying somehow to escape, trying to crawl away, but it's hurt. And the man just keeps kicking it, over and over." She turned her head away from Jude. "I knew who he was, too. He came over to our house with his kids once for a barbeque. I thought he was a nice man."

You go dead inside was what Howard Bisbee had said. Jude thought of trying to reassure Caroline that the barbeque guest might have been a good person, yet inside the slaughterhouse he became someone else. But she wasn't quite sure she could square the two, much less explain to this child whose world had been upended by what she had witnessed.

"Please don't make me go home tonight," begged Caroline.

And Jude didn't.

CHAPTER 26

Well past midnight at the Kings Court park, the trailers looked like rows of shipping containers in the dark. No sounds came from within and even the loose dogs were asleep. Shavings of light appeared at the bottom of the drawn shades at the Vargas trailer, however, where Abelina scurried around in her robe, gathering gauze and antibiotic cream for the wound on Jude's hand. Her medical training was well-known at the trailer park, particularly since so many of the workers were loathe to report their injuries in case they were instructed not to come to work. And like them, Jude counted not only on Abelina's nursing skills, but her discretion. She gritted her teeth as she received her five stitches. Finn lay on the floor of the miniature kitchen. Abelina didn't think his leg was broken, but suggested Jude take him to a vet in the morning. For now, he was quiet, his eyes following Abelina and checking every once in a while to make sure Jude was near. Caroline had crashed on a cot set up in the sitting area; Daniel was somewhere in the neighborhood trying to drum up a computer so Jude could watch the video.

When Abelina was done, Jude called the Chapel home and Emmet picked up. "She's fine, Emmet," said Jude. "But she doesn't want to come home just yet."

"Where was she?" he asked, keeping his voice low so as not to wake his wife.

"She'll tell you," said Jude simply.

"I'll come over and get her."

"No, don't, she's asleep. I'm leaving in the morning. I'll bring her home on the way."

They listened to each other breathe for a moment. While the memory of their earlier intimacy whispered over the line, so did the guilt. Finally Jude said, "Goodbye, Emmet."

Thirty minutes later, she sat by herself at the dinette table and opened the laptop Daniel borrowed from his cousin. He and Abelina had retired to get a few hours sleep before they had to take the baby to a neighbor, then leave for their D&M shifts. Finn was sleeping at her feet, exhausted after his ordeal, his breathing now deep and even. Jude took the disc from its case and examined it, wondering that something so small could have caused so much misery. She inserted it into the drive and waited for the first images to come up.

The picture quality was terrible at first – jerky and often focused a foot or two below what Frank was trying to photograph. Jude guessed that the camera lens had been hidden in a shirt button, and his inexperience was evident in the erratic footage. But he got better as he went along. About two minutes into the video, the stories came alive.

A crew is herding a truckload of hogs into one of the lairage pens. Here's a mound of pig carcasses – the ones who did not survive transport dumped like so much garbage in a heap. Hundreds of flies buzz around them. Two of the pigs are still kicking, one of them at the bottom of the pile. Date stamped: September 9th.

It's now inside the slaughterhouse. Jude can almost feel the oppressive heat and the damp, foul air close in around her. *Two workers run by. A pig is bucking and fighting in the chute. Behind him, traffic is at a standstill and the men are frantic to get it moving, first using an electric prod, then beating it with pipes. The pig collapses on the floor. A white-helmeted worker appears with a large metal hook and he hammers it through the animal's mouth and drags the hog into the stun area. The stunner finally silences the hog's screams.* Date stamped: September 13th.

A pig drops onto the shackling table. With a practiced, fluid motion, the shackler reaches up to the moving rail and pulls down a chain with an alloy hook at the end. Once shackled, the pig is hoisted by its leg and pulled forward. The camera stays on the animal as it regains consciousness. It lifts its head and writhes on the rail until it gets to the sticker, who lunges with his knife. The pig continues to buck as blood pours from its throat. Date stamped: September 14th.

A man has fallen and is scrambling backwards away from the rail, cursing and holding his side. Workers stop what they're doing to look. A figure appears waving his hands in the air and yelling. Keep it going. You, yeah you – get in and replace him – keep it going! The figure turns his face toward the camera. His expression is not of anger, but of fear. He has a thick, white scar running from his cheekbone up into the dark recesses of his helmet. Date stamped: September 21st.

Jude's mouth ran dry as more played out. She fast-forwarded through much of the footage. Hundreds of hogs thundered by, some with open, infected wounds, broken legs, ears or tails chewed off – signs of having been cannibalized in the factory farms. Animal excrement splashed on the tile walls. Men and women with grim faces, blood-soaked up to their elbows, flashing knives. Conscious hogs going up on the chain. Writhing, squealing. Hogs dumped into the scalding tank, some struggling to get out. Of course Jude knew that the industry accepted that a certain percentage of animals would be shackled and bled out while fully conscious, industry standards deemed it acceptable that a certain number went into the scalding tank alive. At D&M it was relentless.

As suddenly as the images had started, the screen went black and it was over. Jude would have stopped the tape and removed the disc, but still in shock, she just sat there. Soon she became aware of muffled sounds and the flickering of dark shadows on the screen. It wasn't over. Heavy breathing and grunting. Was it Frank? If so, he was laboring. He cursed under his breath, his footsteps shuffled on the ground. And then men's voices, dim at first, but getting louder, echoing as if from far away.

She's a beauty. I gotta admit, I'm jealous.

Another man said, *It's got Smart Phone Integration with a roof-mounted antenna that gives you great reception, even when you're out here in the sticks. And this BMW has great re-sale potential if you want to trade it in.*

How much?

Fully loaded ... about seventy-five grand. Hey, it's not out of reach. I was just where you are a few years ago. There's a place for you in corporate, Bob. And it could be sooner rather than later.

Oh yeah?

Listen, I'm going to be spending less of my time in Raleigh and a lot more talking with the folks in Washington. That's where the money is. And once you get in the door to a couple of House members, you can add a lot of value. I'm not saying you'd come into my spot, per se. But there's a regional management job opening up, and that's the first step. I can put you on that list, and I think Seldon would consider you.

Thanks, Ned. Appreciate that.

Squeezing her eyes shut, Jude tried to picture the speakers. "Bob" had to be Bob Warshauer, the plant manager, but who was "Ned?" And then she remembered what Frank had told her about recording a conversation between Warshauer and a rising VP in the corporation. Had to be Ned Bannerman, Marshfield's favored son.

Hey, Bob, we need to talk. Shut the door, okay? Jude leaned in to hear better. *How many head you turning?*

A little more than five hundred an hour.

Yeah, I know. Not enough. We've got three other plants with the same equipment and they're outpacing you.

Warshauer's reply was offered up almost as an apology. *We've tried speeding it up in the last few months, but the workers can't keep up. They quit, they get hurt.*

Train 'em better.

We're always training, but the turnover means I got new people on the line every day. Half of them don't speak English and the other half don't give a crap. You know I can't risk a recall. When we pick up the speed, we have to prod every hog, they get jumpy, don't get stunned right, and more of 'em go up live on the bleed rail. That turns into high injury rates on the floor. I don't need OSHA breathing down my neck.

You running out of folks looking for work?

No, but–

Hey, everybody's in the same boat. You just gotta take the heat. Who's heading up your USDA inspectors? Bannerman was asking.

Patrick LaBrie, and Frank Cimino's the vet in charge.

You on good terms with them?

Yeah, pretty good. It's give and take.

So there's no problem. Look, I know those guys, they're team play-

ers. They used to work over at the Rock Hill facility. You're lucky to have them here. You just worry about the end product, hear? The animals are not talking.

Jude caught herself holding her breath.

Let me lay it out for you, Bannerman was saying. *At forty-six hundred hogs per shift, you'll be in Bragg Falls a long time. At forty-eight ... forty-nine, you've got a ticket to Raleigh.*

That's ... that's close to a hog every six seconds. Jude could almost see the sweat pouring down Warshauer's face.

What can I tell you? That extra five percent is where we beat the competition, it's how we keep the big supermarket chains, and it's how you build your resume. There's only one manager getting that regional job and I'd like it to be you. But you got to give me the numbers. You need one good year.

Yeah, well ... I suppose I can pump up the tally again, but the animals ... the workers ...

Then do it. Like I said, the hogs ain't talkin' and neither are your illegals. You know the margins we work on in this business, it's all about line speed. But there's some things we can't put on paper, which is why I'm here today. Seldon wants me to personally explain to each manager just what it takes so we're on the same page. This is coming straight from Seldon. Line speed, Bob. Line speed.

The voices faded, but Jude had heard all she needed. She pulled out the disc with trembling fingers and immediately secured it deep inside her jacket pocket. Here was proof that at the highest levels Marshfield Industries not only knew about the horrific abuse to the animals and the danger posed to the employees because of the breakneck line speed, they wanted to make it run even faster. This last is what Frank meant when he told her he had recorded "dynamite" – and it's probably what had gotten him killed.

Jude heard a sound just outside the trailer and startled. She

didn't think she'd been followed, but she was still on edge. Whoever had been shooting at Roy Mears was a big unknown. He may
have saved her life and she didn't know why, but it didn't feel like
an altogether well-meaning gesture. She pulled aside the trailer's
homemade curtain and peered through the window. In the pre-
dawn light there was only a feral cat slinking around the corner.
She let the curtain fall back and nervously checked the time. Too
early to call Gordon. He'd want to orchestrate the release of the
video to the media, then prepare for the swift and aggressive corporate response. Marshfield would, of course, claim it was all fabricated by animal rights extremists, but the more they protested, the
more they'd draw attention to the issue. Gordon knew a reporter
at CNN who would broadcast portions of the video. It would get
picked up on Facebook, YouTube, Twitter. Many people wouldn't
want to look, wouldn't want to know. But enough would. Change
was going to come.

CHAPTER 27

Jude drove slowly up the circular driveway and stopped in front of the high school entrance. "Your mom knows I'm dropping you off at school, right?"

"I told her. She's still peeved about last night, so this will give her a little time to cool off."

"You want to call her again?"

"Can't, my battery died. Stupid phone – I just charged it yesterday. But I did call her. Abelina let me use her phone before we left." She reached around to stroke Finn under the chin. "He'll be fine, won't he?"

"I'm going to get him checked out before I head on back. He's pretty sturdy." Jude tried to sound reassuring, but she was worried. Finn was limping badly this morning. "Say, do you, uh, need a note or something? I mean, for being late?"

Caroline smiled – an actual smile that created a dimple in her right cheek. "I think it has to be from a parent or a doctor," she said. "But it would be cool to see what the attendance office thought of a note from an animal rights terrorist."

"Good point," Jude grinned back.

There was an awkward moment as they struggled with how to say their goodbyes. Caroline postponed it by offering, "I've gone vegan, you know."

"Really?"

"Yeah, I've been doing some research on the web and learning about all the foods that come from animals and vegan alternatives and stuff."

"Good for you. How do your folks feel about it?"

Caroline shrugged. "They think it's a phase. But I know it's not. I don't want to be a part of all that." She nodded in the direction of the plant. "Anyway, I can cook for myself."

With only a few hours sleep, there were smoky circles under the girl's eyes, but there was an energy emanating from her that Jude hadn't seen before. She felt an overwhelming desire to protect Caroline from the difficulties she would face in a world that too often equated being a vegan with being an extremist. But the second period bell rang from inside the building, marking the time for a wordless farewell hug.

An x-ray of Finn's back leg revealed no fractures. The local vet diagnosed a severe sprain of his already weakened hip, then treated a few cuts on the pads of his feet. At one point he glanced over to Jude's own bandaged hand, but refrained from asking any questions. She left feeling much relieved and with a prescription for Finn of rest and an aspirin every twelve hours. She called in to Gordon and checked out of the motel. Then, after making Finn comfortable in the back of the Subaru, she was finally heading home.

On her way, Jude drove down Main Street, passing the corner Gulf station, the Hardware & Feed Store, and the rickety building that housed the *Chronicle*. The hard corners of the DVD's plastic case in her pocket poked into her ribcage and made it impossible not to think about the effect the video might have on these businesses and the people who worked there – to Emmet and Caroline, Howard Bisbee, and all the other workers and their families dependent on a vast profit-driven industry that keeps upping the ante on the backs of helpless animals and desperate workers. Whatever the impact, Jude knew it was right to release this new evidence, proof of Marshfield's moral corruption. As it was, going up against the meat industry's money, power and political influence was like David fighting Goliath. Now finally, she had a weapon worthy of the battlefield, and she knew that she ought to feel good. Still, something weighed heavily on her and she couldn't put her finger on it.

"Hi, CJ." Jude put her phone on speaker as she drove.

"Where are you?" he wanted to know. "What's going on?"

"I'm on my way back."

"How's Finn?"

"He's going to be fine, but he's not walking too well. Just have to keep him quiet for a few days."

"We'll take good care of him here. Hey, Gordon filled us in this morning. You've got the video. That's huge."

"Yeah, it's going to change the dialogue, guaranteed."

"Mmn, your words are saying one thing, your voice is telling me something else. Are you alright?" asked CJ.

"I keep thinking about what happened at the house where we rescued Finn. Did Gordon tell you about that?"

"He said someone stopped that guy Mears from shooting you, so I see that as a positive."

"But I can't put it together. I was under the impression that the folks in Bragg Falls would've been just as happy if Mears did shoot me. Someone prevented him from doing that, which meant they must have followed me there, and I'm usually better at spotting a tail. I feel like there's this great big puzzle surrounding Frank and the tape, and I'm just a small piece in it."

After a moment, CJ said, "What if ... this protective shadow wasn't looking out for *you*, but for Caroline or Jack?"

"But nobody knew they were there."

"Nobody except for whoever it was that showed up and kept Mears from killing you all."

"I don't understand."

But the answer came to Jude just as CJ voiced it. "Didn't Caroline have the video? Maybe they knew that and didn't want anything to happen to *her*."

"Until they got their hands on it," finished Jude.

"It's a theory."

"But ... but how could they know she had the tape? She and Sophie were very secretive, and Caroline didn't have it in her hands until yesterday."

"Could have bugged her house or phone, I guess."

The pieces of the puzzle began to fly together. "Oh, God," Jude said aloud. "Caroline told me earlier that she couldn't call home because her phone had run out of battery. For a teenage girl that's pretty unlikely, isn't it? And I remember that the first time I met Verna, she was distraught over the fact that she'd tried to reach Frank the night he died, but she couldn't get through because she said his phone was always running out of battery ... CJ, are you still there?"

"I'm here," he said, his voice unusually somber.

"Do you think they bugged Frank's phone?" asked Jude, already knowing the answer.

CJ was a step ahead of her. "Spyware on a phone drains the battery real quick," he prefaced. "They could have gotten to Frank's phone in his locker or taken it from his car while he was at work. Spyware is easy enough to put on."

"And they'd be able to listen in on his calls?" asked Jude.

"Are you kidding?" snorted CJ. "Listen to his calls, track the numbers he dialed, pinpoint his location on GPS, read his texts. Hell, with the right equipment, they could *send* him phony texts."

"That's how they knew." Jude's eyes were watching the road, but in her mind, she was visualizing the dark forces of Marshfield's damage control suiting up for battle. "Somebody at the plant reported seeing Frank with a camera and they bugged his phone. That's how they knew he'd made the tape and contacted us. And they were listening when Frank told me he'd recorded a conversation between Warshauer and Bannerman ... one that implicated Seldon Marshfield." The next conclusion was painful to voice. "They would've known when I was coming down to meet Frank, and they got rid of him before I could get here."

"Jesus," muttered CJ. "And you're saying that Caroline's phone has been acting up as well? Why would they tag *her* phone?"

"I'm not sure," Jude responded. "Maybe they had the whole Marino family bugged. Maybe they got to Caroline because of her friendship with me. They've got plenty of resources to cast a wide net. Of course, it's so bloody ironic because Frank didn't make a copy – it was the girls who did it on the sly."

The connection Jude made next made her stomach heave. If Marshfield was reading Caroline's cell phone texts, then the last thing they'd seen before her battery ran down was that she had the video. *Sophie's so pissed. She's been sending me mad texts all night. I shouldn't have taken it today, but I had to.*

The entrance to the highway lay ahead. "I gotta go," said Jude. She tossed her cell phone on the seat next to her and hauled on the steering wheel to make the u-turn.

CHAPTER 28

As Jude raced back toward Bragg Falls, self-recrimination rolled over her in waves. So much she had missed. True, she couldn't have foreseen that two teenage girls would make a copy of Frank's video, but she should have seen beyond Caroline's infatuation ... following her to the ridge at D&M, inviting her to dinner where she'd probably planned to say something about the video. Caroline had been trying to connect for a reason and Jude missed it. Just as negligent, she had underestimated Marshfield. Did she really think they wouldn't search under every rock, in every corner and on every cell phone until they were satisfied that no copy existed? She'd been so focused on what the video meant to the animal movement that she missed what it meant to Marshfield. So filled with hope about shining a light on the company's abusive practices that she missed their laser beam trained on a girl who only wanted to help – a girl who had risked her life to rescue Finn.

It seemed obvious now that the "protective shadow," as CJ had referred to him, was there to safeguard Caroline from Roy Mears.

He needed her alive to lead him to the videotape she had taken from Sophie. Jude had little doubt that he would find her again – and quickly. What he would do when he found her, Jude didn't know.

She had to get to Caroline first.

The high school was just letting out. Jude tried to position herself where she could see the crowd of teenagers pouring out of the building and onto the yellow buses lined up around the circular driveway. She craned her neck looking for Caroline's gangly gait. One by one, the buses loaded up and pulled away, and the stream of students diminished to a trickle. Where was she?

She spotted Sophie emerge and walk purposefully toward the last bus, which started its engine as she approached. Jude hurried over, meeting Sophie at the steps of the bus.

"Do you know where Caroline is?" asked Jude hurriedly.

Sophie's eyes widened in surprise and she shook her head no.

Jude's heart began to flutter in panic. "She was in school though, right?"

"Uh, yeah."

"I need to find her. Is she still inside?"

"No, she left."

Jude grabbed Sophie by the shoulders. "Where did she go?"

"She went running."

"Running?"

"Yeah, she was going on her long run … to clear her head."

"Where?"

"In the park somewhere." Sophie lifted her eyes to the hill that rose up behind the football field.

"When?" cried Jude. "When did she leave?"

"Right after class. A few minutes ago."

The bus driver called to Sophie; she was holding everybody up. Jude let her go.

She knew where Caroline was headed and only hoped that she could find the trail again – the trail that led to a spot high up where a troubled young girl could clear her head, to a place that was *clean and pure*.

Jude dashed back to the car and drove it around to the parking lot next to the football field where a group of boys were suiting up with shoulder pads, readying themselves for practice. One stood apart from the others, balancing himself on crutches and joking around with his fellow teammates. Jude trotted up to him.

"I'll pay you twenty dollars to keep an eye on my dog," she said breathlessly. Finn could not be with her, not now. He would try to keep up with her and might hurt himself further. Not this time. "He can stay in the car over there. Just make sure no one lets him out."

The kid didn't have to be asked twice. "Sure," he said, pointing to the cast on his leg, "I'm not goin' anywhere."

Jude dug in her wallet for the cash. She cracked the windows and locked the car. "Is there a trail that goes up into the park from here?" she asked, pressing the money into the boy's hand.

"The track team uses one that starts behind that goalpost."

"Okay, thanks."

"Say, listen," he said. "Practice goes 'til six. You'll be back by then?"

Jude mumbled an affirmative answer, but she was already running.

The path was wide and climbed slowly, and keeping up a steady trot wasn't difficult. Then Jude came to a fork where a narrower trail continued to ascend. Yellow circles painted on the trees marked it as the one that led to the ridge where Jude had first met Caroline. Without hesitation, Jude continued the climb.

Quickly the terrain changed. Exposed roots and mossy rocks littered the path, forcing Jude to slow her pace or risk a sprained ankle. In a matter of minutes, she was breathing hard and sweating underneath her jacket. But she pushed forward. Before long, she found herself trudging along the side of a ridge where gunmetal sky and glimpses of hilltops came into view. And up ahead the ground opened up to a familiar scenic overlook.

Caroline was standing on a slab of rock, framed by the distant hills, charcoal blue in the late afternoon haze. But in the clearing between them stood a man with his back to Jude. He and Caroline appeared to be in the middle of an argument, because Caroline's face was red with anger. "Who the fuck *are* you?" she demanded brashly.

He answered her softly, evenly, and Jude couldn't quite hear what he said. But she knew why he was there. "Let her go," she called out. "I have what you want."

He whipped around, pointing a gun at her chest. Behind the non-descript, pleasant features, he assessed her with the calculating gaze of someone who wouldn't think twice about killing her and a meddling teenage girl. There was no doubt in Jude's mind that he worked for Marshfield and that there would never be any proof of that.

"Look who's here," he said with the barest of smiles.

"She doesn't have the video," announced Jude. "She gave it to me."

Bloom swiveled his head between the two, then motioned Jude with the barrel of his gun over to where Caroline stood.

As Jude cautiously complied, she held up her hands and said, "I'm not armed as I'm sure you know. I'm going to hand it over nice and slow." She pulled out the disc from her pocket and held it out to him.

"No!" cried Caroline.

Later, Jude recalled hearing defiance in her voice, but in the moment she thought it was a cry of despair at being forced to concede. And perhaps the man heard the same thing because he lowered his gun. In that instant Caroline snatched the disc from Jude's hand and darted to the edge of the cliff. She scrambled over the wooden railing and positioned herself on the narrow, rocky ledge of the precipice, holding out her arms for balance.

"You're not getting this," she threatened, raising the disc aloft. "If you come near me, I'll jump."

Bloom stopped in his tracks and a flicker of uncertainty passed over his face. In it Jude saw his dilemma. If Caroline took the disc over the edge, it might well withstand the fall, even if the girl didn't. But with cops combing the hillside for her body, he could scarcely stick around to try and find it.

Jude reached out her hand. "Caroline, please don't," she implored.

"No. You need it. You need it ... to help the animals."

"Don't do it, Caroline."

"I don't care. I don't want to live in a world that treats animals so badly." She began to sob. "You'll be able to show people..."

"I understand, but–"

"They're just innocent *animals*. And they're suffering so much." Caroline's foot slipped on a loose piece of gravel and she lurched, but managed to right herself again.

Jude's heart was pounding. The slightest movement might startle the girl off balance again – even more frightening, she might say the wrong thing and it would only strengthen Caroline's resolve to jump. So many times Jude herself felt that she was teetering on the edge of reason – times that she bore witness to so much agony that the world seemed insane for not seeing it as well, and she didn't know where or how she could fit in. Words of reassurance and hope had never been enough. Maybe the only lifeline for Caroline was the truth, something her family and community had tried to shield her from.

"Then help them," said Jude. "Stay alive and help them."

"How? No one's listening!" screamed Caroline.

"I am. *I'm* listening. And others will, too. But it will take more than one video. We have to keep fighting and we need your help. We have to reach people even when they don't want to listen. When they toss your leaflets on the ground, you have to pick them up and hand them to the next person. You protest and boycott, and when the corporations shut you down, you fight harder. You investigate, you expose, you educate. Sometimes I stay awake at night thinking about all the suffering animals bred and raised just to be slaughtered, and sometimes it makes me feel like things will never change. But I wake up and do it all again the next day. It's hard work, Caroline. And there aren't many of us, which is why we need you."

Caroline's body stiffened, but in her eyes Jude saw the emergence of a new light – a spark of understanding.

Jude reached out her hand again, urging her back into the world. "There is no other choice," she said. "You don't get to surrender!"

With a final look over her shoulder, Caroline turned back and ready to come forward from her precarious perch, she held out the video to Jude.

But neither of them had seen Bloom inch ever so slowly forward. And finally, when he was close enough, he leapt toward Caroline and seized the video from her outstretched hand. His sudden movement so startled her that she put up both hands in an instinctive reaction and lost her balance. Her arms flailed and she grasped at the railing. At one time it might have held, but on such an untraveled path, no ranger had bothered to climb up and replace the rotting boards. Now, too weak to support her, the railing gave way with a sickening crack. She went over the edge with an anguished howl.

Jude could have sworn she saw Marshfield's man make a stab to keep her from falling, but it all happened so fast. As Jude rushed forward, hearing her own scream echoing that of Caroline's, Bloom turned and punched her hard across the side of the face. Everything turned to dizzying pinpoints of light, then went black before she hit the ground.

CHAPTER 29

The nurse screeched the dividing curtain closed, leaving Jude alone in the cubicle at last. Between the x-rays, nurses, hospital administrators, and the Sheriff's people, she hadn't had a moment to herself. She reached up to touch the painful lump at her temple where Bloom's fist had landed. Her entire head throbbed, but she had gotten off lucky. More importantly, she was able to say the same thing about Caroline who, all in all, was fortunate to be alive.

Jude didn't know how long she'd been unconscious, maybe a few minutes, maybe half an hour. Slowly she became aware of the pain in her head, the uneven, frozen ground digging into her back, and the sound of a lone hawk, cawing, circling above her. Then she remembered and forced herself upright. She staggered to the spot where Caroline had fallen. The plunge appeared perilously steep, but Jude located a path that wound down from the summit among bushes and small trees that grew out of the rocky slope. They had prevented Caroline's fall from being fatal. Jude scrambled down, slipping and sliding, hanging on to anything she could to keep from tumbling to the bottom, until she found Caroline. Scrapes and scratches criss-crossed her legs and face, and one arm was a twisted mess underneath her. But very much alive and dimly conscious, she began to weep when she saw Jude.

It took nearly forty minutes for the paramedics to get her out by helicopter. Because she had to get back to Finn, Jude declined the air lift and walked back with two deputies. The next couple of hours were a blur of questions. Grady Ward had come to the emergency room while Jude was waiting to be tended. She had misjudged him. He was still a cop with a job to do, but his underlying gentleness moved her. He shared what information he had, which wasn't much. Based on the description Jude had given, a statewide bulletin of the person she insisted on referring to as "Marshfield's man" had been broadcast, airports and train stations monitored, but so far there had been no sighting. Jude didn't think there would be.

She went over and over the events of the past several days, sticking with her unwavering belief that the man was an operative for the giant meat company and that he had come to Bragg Falls to get Frank's video. But she had no hard evidence to connect him to the corporation or to Frank's death, and Marshfield's legal team was denying any knowledge of the whole affair. Indeed, they wanted to help, even offering a monetary reward for the capture of the man who had allegedly terrorized a child of one of their employees. Still, one of the lawyers had not so subtly previewed their case, already having learned that the young witness was on medication and seeing a psychiatrist – clearly psychologically unstable "before this terrible tragedy."

"Can I see her?" Jude asked Ward.

He shook his head. "She's in surgery," he advised.

Jude was finally cleared to leave. She walked through the sitting area of the ER, where sickness and worry filled the chairs. Several people were waiting to be admitted and others glanced up, anxiously hoping for news about a loved one. They looked as hopeless and lost as Jude felt. As she went through the swinging doors to the outside, she crossed paths with Alice Chapel. The two women locked gazes. Alice turned her head sharply away, but not before Jude caught the full brunt of the accusation in her eyes. It hurt worse than the throbbing ache in her head and sent her blindly out into the early dusk.

She'd declined Ward's offer to have one of his deputies take her back to Bragg Falls where Finn was staying with an animal control officer and insisted she could take a cab. But rather than waiting at the hospital entrance, she went across the street to a small municipal park, quite empty since it was only meant as ornamental landscaping. There she found a bench to sit down. She pulled her knees up to her chest and let the tears come. This failure felt so much worse than anything she had known before. A young girl badly hurt. Almost killed. Probably no way of finding who had terrorized them and in all likelihood killed Frank Marino. And now, of course, she had no ammunition against Marshfield, no way to stop what was going on at D&M – a place so dark that even God's grace could not find a way in, or so Verna Marino believed. Was that the definition of hell, Jude wondered?

"Jude."

She looked up to see Emmet standing in front of her. For a moment, she thought he had come to offer comfort, but his face was ravaged with anger. "Why don't you just get the fuck away from here," he burst out.

Brushing her cheeks dry, Jude said, "I'm sorry. I never meant for this to happen."

"You've brought nothing good. Nothing but hurt. You and your high-minded ideals."

"Emmet, I never meant–"

"Frank Marino died because of you."

"That's not fair, Emmet. I never asked him to make a video."

"You encouraged him. Made him feel like he was making such a great moral sacrifice. All you people want to do is pursue your animal agenda and to hell with the rest of us. And now my little girl is lying up there, all broken to bits. That maniac didn't want her. He wanted *you*. Goddamn it, he should have pushed you off the cliff instead of her!"

Jude jumped up. "Is that what you think happened?"

He didn't answer.

"For your information, he did not push Caroline off. I think he ... he might have tried to catch her, but she was the one who climbed onto that ledge. She threatened to jump." The color left his cheeks. "She didn't want to give it to him. She threatened to take the disc to the bottom with her."

"What? What the hell are you talking about?"

"The disc ... the video." Jude then realized that the police hadn't yet told him. "The girls found Frank's video weeks ago. They made a copy."

"I ... don't understand. Caroline *saw* all that footage?" Somehow that seemed as frightening to him as the thought of her devastating fall.

"Yeah, Emmet, she did." Jude's bottled up frustration and anger erupted. "You don't get it, do you? All you see is standard industry procedure and the paycheck that comes with it, just like all you see is what your daughter is *supposed* to look like. Caroline and Sophie found Frank's video, and what they saw in the slaughterhouse terrified them. It would any kid. And how could Caroline come to you? How could she even tell you? You're a part of it … more than a part, you're in the driver's seat." Jude couldn't help herself, even recognizing that she was digging the hole in Emmet's heart a little deeper with each accusation. "She saw a man beating a pig to death on the floor – the same man who had come to your house for a barbeque … like it's all *normal,* like torturing and killing animals is just part of everyday life.

"She saw *you* in the video, Emmet. She was horrified. And when she cuts off her hair and suddenly breaks all your rules – a way of telling you how confused she is, you want to squeeze her back into a restraining device. When she tries to tell you how painful it is, you put her on drugs because you can't stand to hear the screams. And when she fights back, you punish her, just like you punish all the hogs who won't willingly march to their death. Is it any wonder she feels like one of them?"

Emmet buried his head in his hands and an agonized groan escaped from deep in his chest. She didn't regret lashing out at him, but unable to bear any more pain, Jude turned and walked away.

* * *

Emmet perched at the edge of a metal chair in the dimly lit room where his daughter lay. Her eyes were closed and she was still, but the silent drip of the IV and the pulsing green lines on the machine next to the bed were life-affirming. He pulled close to the side of the bed and gently held her hand. The pain killer was sending her in and out of a hazy, tormented sleep. Emmet waited, listening to the sounds of the busy corridor outside her room.

"Daddy?" Her eyelids fluttered.

"I'm here, honey," he said, pulling his chair closer.

She croaked, "Daddy, I'm sorry."

Emmet reached up and began to stroke the hair from her face, careful not to catch his rough fingers on her multiple earrings. "No, no, you have nothing to be sorry about, honey," he said softly. "It's me who's sorry."

"Dad?" Her voice sounded far away. "Will you be angry if I tell you something?"

"Of course not."

"I want to fight for the animals. I want to do what Jude is doing." She seemed to drift off again.

"Okay, okay, honey. You rest," he hushed. "I'll be here."

As her breathing deepened, Emmet leaned his forehead on the cool sheets by her outstretched arm and prayed for the first time since he had intoned the Lord's Prayer at Frank's gravesite. But the words came out in a prayer of gratitude not to God but to his daughter. "Thank you, Caroline," whispered. "Thank you for staying alive ... thank you for having the will to live. You can fight for the animals, you can be a vegetarian, you can be anything you want. Just give me another chance. I'll make it up to you, I swear."

Before he lifted his head, he knew what he had to do.

CHAPTER 30

The last transport of the morning had finished unloading. Crammed into the lairage pen, the sows were coated in layers of dirt and manure; they jostled against one another, trying to break free, but had no place to go. Emmet stepped out into the yard to oversee this next group going through. Even with all the activity, the yard seemed almost quiet without Crank. There was a new man in his place. Emmet called out a few unnecessary instructions; the line was moving well. Lately, there seemed to be many more breeding sows coming through. Emmet had heard it was part of a culling program to keep industry prices up. This group didn't look very healthy, though. They were worn out, many with open wounds from rubbing against the bars of their crates. But they weren't fighting and that made everyone's job easier. Fitting his earplugs back in, he returned to the kill floor.

Things weren't going quite as smoothly inside. They were down a sticker and Howard Bisbee had to fill in. The hesitant Hispanic stunner replacing Tim Vernon had learned the routine, but didn't have the malicious confidence of his predecessor. Emmet thought his name was José, but couldn't be sure. He took a moment to see if the kid had improved his technique. José had a split second to adjust the handles of the stunning device, twisting them to just the right angle. The next sow came through the chute, its body squeezed between the panels, its legs dangling helplessly. José held the tongs on either side of the pig's head. Zzzp! The pig went down. Six seconds later another one came through. Zzzp! Same result. One by one they dropped onto the wide shackle table for the next step in the dis-assembly line. Every third or fourth animal, however, José didn't manage to get the stunner in the proper position, with no time to get the tongs placed just right for a good stun. When that happened, the hog would buck and thrash, and the young stunner would go in for another jolt, hitting it again, and sometimes a third time.

This wasn't good. Emmet hollered at him to do a better job and trotted down to where the shacklers were working. There were already two sows in the pit below the table. If a hog wasn't stunned properly, they were supposed to let it hit the floor; someone else had to come with a portable machine and re-stun it. When the shackler saw Emmet, he re-doubled his efforts, knowing that if there were too many in the pit, his supervisor would write him up. Under pressure, however, the shackler hoisted two sows that showed signs of consciousness.

The chain was moving faster than ever. Each man at his station worked feverishly, hands, feet, moving all the time. To Emmet they looked like dull-eyed pieces of a single engine – all part of the chain that turned animals into meat and men into soulless cogs in an unstoppable machine.

Suddenly, he heard shouting down the line. Emmet raced over and saw Howard Bisbee on his knees, his face contorted in a grimace. A sow had struck out with her hoof and kicked him as she went by. While a couple of workers pulled Bisbee back, Emmet followed the sow. Blood gushed from her neck, but she was still bucking and swaying on the rail, trying to lift her head. She squealed in terror. Emmet had to make a quick decision. Bisbee had already missed two more. And they just kept coming.

Emmet leaned down and grabbed the knife from Bisbee's hand. He chased down the sow, now writhing so violently on the chain she had dislocated her shackled leg. Just as he positioned the knife, she lifted her head and looked directly at him. Her dark, liquid eyes were filled with such sadness and pleading, he almost couldn't do it. "Forgive me," he whispered, then plunged the knife in her throat, feeling the last of him break.

The sow went into a final spasm and swung away. Emmet dropped the knife on the floor and lurched over to the red emergency button on the wall behind him. He slammed his palm, slick with the sow's blood, against it. Three blasts from an alarm sounded throughout the building and before the last one faded, the rail had screeched to a halt. In the absence of its incessant noise came the sounds of bellowing hogs, the hissing of the scalding tank, and workers calling out to alert the line further down. Bisbee was trying to get to his feet, inspecting the place where the sharp hoof had rent his heavy apron and opened up a gash in his thigh.

"You okay?" asked Emmet.

He nodded.

"Go down to the medical office and get someone to take you to the hospital."

Bisbee attempted a protest, but Emmet said, "Just do it." He turned to the faces that stared at him, waiting for his next move. "All right, listen up everyone," he called out. "I want every hog in the chute returned to the pens. Don't try to back them up. Open the chute and let them out on the floor – even outside – if you have to." He pointed to the newbie stunner who stood wide-eyed. "What's your name?" asked Emmet.

"Hector."

"Okay, Hector, take the portable, go down this line and make sure that every pig on the rail is stunned properly. I'll go with you to finish the job." The men looked at him as though he had lost his mind.

No one moved. *Return the pigs to the yard? Open the chute?* What he was asking was bizarre and they were afraid to comply.

Emmet shouted, "I am the fucking floor supervisor. Just do it, now!"

Jumping into action, Hector hurried to get the portable stunner and Emmet retrieved Bisbee's knife. They went down the line one by one, finishing off each of the hanging sows that might still be alive. Someone in the back had opened the chute and others were driving pigs back toward the holding pens; a few of the pigs had escaped and were running around the kill floor. This was the scene that met Bob Warshauer when he stormed into the area with Lawrence Cimino at his side.

"What the hell is going on?" Warshauer demanded. "Who stopped the chain?"

"I did," said Emmet, examining the last hog by the scalding tank.

Warshauer was furious. "Why'd you stop it?"

"One of my workers got hurt," Emmet said, walking up to confront him.

"How bad?"

"He'll live, but I sent him to the hospital."

"Then what the fuck are you doing, Chapel? The line stops for emergencies only."

"A man is hurt. We've got conscious pigs going up on the chain. They're getting tossed into the tank and boiled alive," Emmet shot back. "That's an emergency."

Cimino put his hand out in a placating gesture. "Come on, Emmet, don't confuse reflexive movements with consciousness."

"The doctor's right," Warshauer remonstrated. "And if that ever did happen, you tell Cimino and he'll write it up."

A voice over by the shackling table muttered, "That'll be the day."

After shooting a glare in that direction, Warshauer barked, "Get the line going. We can figure this out later." He turned to go back upstairs.

"No. The chain has stopped for today," said Emmet. When his boss whipped back around, he went on, "It's gone on too long. The animals suffer, the workers are treated like shit. You and your bosses all the way up to Raleigh know it. The USDA knows it. And nobody will do a goddamn thing."

"You're out of line, Chapel!" Warshauer pointed his finger in Emmet's face.

Emmet angrily swiped Warshauer's hand away from his face. "Like Frank Marino was out of line?" he challenged. "*Out of line* when he made the video? *Out of line* when you found out he was going to turn it over to an animal welfare group? Is that why you had him killed?"

Warshauer's face went slack, but he stood his ground. "How dare you accuse me. You're crazy."

As if to affirm that he was indeed, Emmet held his knife up to Warshauer's throat. "And then when you found out my daughter had a copy of the video, you sent someone to kill her."

"I ... don't know what you're talking about," stammered Warshauer. "I don't know anything about any copy."

Inching the knife closer, Emmet said, "I could kill you right here on the floor, hang you up with the pigs and never think twice. And it wouldn't be the first time it crossed my mind."

"Get a grip, Chapel. I don't know what happened with your daughter or with Frank Marino. You got nothing on me." Knowing Emmet's hands were tied in front of so many witnesses, Warshauer warned, "Now, get the fuck out of here. You're fired!"

Emmet stared at him for a moment longer, then slowly put the knife on the floor. But instead of doing as he was told, he began to unbutton his coveralls and said, "Fine by me. But we're going down together." He wrenched open the front of the uniform to reveal adhesive tape strapped around his torso – holding in place a small camera and microphone.

"You sonofabitch!" exclaimed Warshauer. He grabbed for the camera, but Emmet slapped his hand away. Red-faced, the plant manager pointed to a worker standing a few feet from Emmet and ordered, "You, get that camera from him."

The worker offered an apologetic shrug and said, "No hablo Ingles."

Wheeling around, Warshauer shouted to the group of men who had gathered. "Somebody take that goddamn camera!"

No one made a move. Not until Emmet turned to leave, and then the men silently stepped back and opened a path for him. He walked past a few pigs still loose in the passageway to the holding pens; behind him Warshauer was screaming to start the line again. Once outside, Emmet stripped off the camera and went around the building to the parking lot where a knot of reporters waited. His hands shook with emotion and more than a little fear. The future he thought he had was gone in an instant, leaving in its place a daunting, blank emptiness. But he felt like an honest man – and that was enough.

The female reporter from WXTO, a local television station, was the first to thrust a microphone in his face. "Mr. Chapel, you alerted our producer that there are serious violations of the law going on at this plant. What kind of violations?"

He cleared his throat. "Uh, violations of the Humane Slaughter Act for one."

"What is that?"

"It's a federal law meant to ensure that the pigs and cows that we slaughter in this country are killed humanely."

Another reporter shouted, "And you're saying that they're not at D&M?"

"Not all of them, no."

"Why is that?"

"Because companies like Marshfield care only about their profits and how they get them doesn't really factor in." Emmet stood taller, his confidence growing. "Here at D&M, the faster the hogs are slaughtered, the more money the company makes. That means we have to keep the line speed going so fast the workers can't keep up. The animals pay a steep price for that and so do the workers who are getting injured every day."

"Workers are injured *every day*?" one called out.

"That's right. Go ahead and look it up. The fact is in any slaughterhouse, the injury rate is about triple that of other manufacturing and processing jobs. And it's not just physical injury. There's even worse damage to the insides of people."

"Where is the USDA?" shouted another.

"You'd have to ask them."

The first reporter moved in to stand next to Emmet so her video crew could get them both on film. "How long have the terrible working conditions been going on at D&M, Mr. Chapel?"

"As long as I can remember, and I've been here a long time."

"You say you have proof of these abuses?" asked the woman.

"Yeah," he said, handing the minicam to her. "The stuff that's on here, it's just a few days, but that's pretty much how it goes all the time ... except for the last part ... what I said to the plant manager. But I'll swear in a court of law that what you'll see in the rest of the video is not in any way unusual."

He looked beyond the reporter to Jude who stood at the back of the group, observing quietly, but with a luminousness that was hard to conceal. She gave Emmet a nod of encouragement and he took strength from it as the reporters shouted out more questions. Emmet Chapel, after all, was the story.

"You're a supervisor at D&M?" asked one.

"Not any more."

"Why are you coming forward now, Mr. Chapel?

"I made a promise to my daughter. And to a friend named Frank Marino."

"If it's as bad as you say, why did you wait so long?"

The question caught him off guard and he looked up for Jude, hoping she would steady him. But like the day at Frank's burial when she had watched him from the top of the hill then disappeared like an apparition, she was gone.

"Mr. Chapel, why did you wait so long?" repeated the newscaster.

Emmet looked directly at her and said, "I don't know. But I'm here now."

EPILOGUE

Alice lugged the last box from the kitchen out to the driveway where Emmet and Howard Bisbee were loading the trailer. Will sat cross legged on the bare living room floor watching TV, the only thing that kept him from getting under foot. The girls wanted a few last moments together, so Sophie and Caroline had meandered out to the yard behind the house where they could be alone.

Back in the kitchen, Verna was busy wiping the counters with a damp rag.

"Don't worry about that," said Alice, returning to see if she'd gotten everything packed.

"Oh, I have to keep busy," replied Verna, "so I don't cry. How do you think the girls will do?"

"It's a big change, but kids are pretty resilient," said Alice. "As soon as we're settled, Sophie can come and visit. And you know them ... they'll be on the phone or texting every day."

The two women could see the girls out the window. "Does Caroline ever talk about it all?" asked Verna.

"Not much with us. But I think Dr. Ohler has been helpful. She seems to be doing much better. She's stopped having these morbid fantasies. She's focused on school again and doing well. Claims she wants to be an animal rights lawyer so she has to get good grades to get into law school. Heck, she's gotten the whole family to give up meat one day a week." Alice touched her friend's shoulder kindly. "How about you and Sophie? This has just been such a terribly difficult time."

"It has. I miss Frank every moment of every day."

"Have you talked to Grady Ward?" asked Alice.

"Not recently. It's an active case and he insists they'll stay on it, but in all honesty, he's probably not going to find out who killed Frank. Even if they did catch the man, they have no proof. The video has disappeared and Marshfield is claiming it never existed."

"But you saw parts of it, and the girls saw it."

Verna shook her head. "I don't know that I'd want the whole thing dredged up again. Sophie feels bad enough as it is."

"Caroline would testify."

"Oh, Alice," said Verna sadly. "It would all boil down to the company's word against that of a traumatized young girl and an animal activist."

At the mention of Jude, Verna saw a hint of pain in Alice's eyes. "What about you and Emmet?" she asked. "Are you going to be okay?"

"Yes, I think so." Alice offered her friend a brave smile. "How long do you think you'll stay?"

"Only until we can sell the house. Then we're going to Florida to live with my cousin until we figure something out."

Emmet poked his head into the kitchen to signal the final boarding call. The last weeks without alcohol and without the daily doses of self-loathing had put color back in his face. Money worries clenched his jaw at night and the decision to leave Bragg Falls had been difficult, but he was facing the hard choices head-on and because of that, a future felt more possible than not.

"Hey Dad!" Will called. "You're on TV!"

The adults headed into the living room, where the five o'clock news was in progress. The anchor on WXTO swiveled to face the camera with an expression of practiced concern. *We're back now with a follow-up story from Jim Howell, who's again on the scene at the D&M pork processing facility in North Carolina. I warn you, some of the images you will see are graphic.*

The eager young reporter took the screen with microphone in hand. *Just four weeks ago, the workers at a meat packing plant in Bragg Falls ... in other words, a slaughterhouse, staged a walkout. Led by a floor supervisor named Emmet Chapel, the workers attested to conditions inside the plant that may surprise you and also make you think twice about where your bacon is coming from.* They played the clip of Emmet speaking to reporters outside the plant, then showed the footage he had taken of conscious sows getting shackled and pulled along the chain. Excerpts from on-site interviews with Howard Bisbee and two other workers followed before the reporter returned to the screen. *The media coverage of the walkout certainly got the attention of Marshfield Industries, which owns this facility. So we're here today in Raleigh to learn more. I'm speaking with Ned Bannerman, the Regional Vice President at Marshfield.*

Along with his custom made Italian suit, Bannerman wore an expression of having been wronged in some way. He leaned into the microphone, saying, *We're deeply distressed about what we saw on the video. We want to ensure our valued customers that this is an isolated incident and is in no way representative of how we conduct business at Marshfield. We have fired the individuals responsible for these incidents. Marshfield has zero tolerance for these actions.*

Howell asked, *Didn't the USDA temporarily shut down the plant?*

It was a joint decision, responded Bannerman, acknowledging a bespectacled man standing next to him. *We wanted to conduct a full review and institute additional training procedures for our employees. But I'm pleased to say that after our review, we are ready to bring D&M up to full speed again. The number of USDA inspectors has been increased, and we will assist them in every way possible.*

Pushing the mic closer, Howell said, *But Mr. Bannerman, I understand that some of the things we heard from the workers about the treatment of the animals and the difficult working conditions are considered standard industry practice. Can you comment?*

The U.S. Department of Agriculture has set stringent regulations that must and will be followed, Bannerman said with finality.

Joining us is George McAlister from the USDA, said Howell, pushing the microphone over to the man with glasses. *Question for you, sir ... Do those regulations include monitoring how fast the hogs are pushed through? And doesn't the line speed impact the working conditions inside?*

McAlister cleared his throat. *We are in the process of reviewing the impact that line speed has on the federal requirements of the Humane Slaughter Act. When our report is finalized, we'll make it publicly available.*

Putting up his hand, Bannerman signaled that the interview was over. He and McAlister began to walk away, but the reporter asked, *Mr. Bannerman, who sets the line speed?*

Bannerman didn't respond, and Jim Howell started after him, calling out more aggressively, *Mr. Bannerman, who sets the line speed?*

The Regional VP stopped and turned. Through a tight smile, he replied, *We will ensure that all state and federal regulations are being followed without exception. At Marshfield, we are dedicated to humane treatment and safe working conditions and to bringing affordable and healthy food to the American dining table.*

"Miss, is that it?" asked the kid behind the register.

His voice startled Jude away from the television mounted on the wall of the mini-mart. "Yes, thanks." She paid cash for the full tank of gas and a package of trail mix for the road, hesitating one last moment to see if they returned to Emmet's interview, but the news station was on to the next segment.

Jude was encouraged that the USDA representative had stated publicly that the agency would be studying line speed, and she hoped that Jim Howell would continue to cover the story – if only to keep the pressure on Marshfield. But as Gordon had impressed upon his staff, they shouldn't entertain illusions that the walkout and subsequent media coverage would change how the industry operated ... the war would wage on.

Indeed, back in Washington, Gordon had her working with a new investigator, teaching him the ropes and creating a back story for him before he ventured into the field. She'd had a chance to catch up with the other investigators, air out her stuffy apartment, and ensure that Finn's leg healed up. Now she was on the road again.

Back in the car, she opened the file that laid out her next assignment: venturing into the wintry world of hunters and trappers out west. Jude tried to re-read the background that CJ had put together, but images of Emmet kept playing in her head. She'd heard the family was moving to California.

Family. The word filled her with longing.

Jude tried to push the feelings away as she pulled out onto the county road. She hadn't been west in a while. She might take a side trip to visit an old college friend after this investigation. The car gathered speed and they traveled past an open field where a flock of birds whirled in circles against the purple glow of dusk. Rolling down the windows, she breathed in the scent of damp hay and the promise of snow. And she reminded herself that hers was a different kind of family – a kinship with innocent pigs heading to slaughter, with hens and cows, wolves, bears, tigers, elephants, dolphins, the vanishing, the voiceless.

She looked over as Finn stuck his head out the window, pointing his nose into the wind. The stream of air ruffled his lips and lifted the flaps of his ears. He looked like he was flying.

Made in the USA
Charleston, SC
28 September 2013